DEAR WRITER

DEAR WRITER

STORIES THAT JUST WEREN'T A GOOD FIT
AT THE TIME

Edited by
Jason Gong &
Alan Good

MAL
ARKEY
BOOKS
DENVER

Malarkey Books
PO Box 19713
Denver CO 80219

Malarkeybooks.com
@MalarkeyBooks

ISBN: 978-0-9981710-8-1

Cover design by Stuart Buck.
@stuartmbuck

TABLE OF CONTENTS

INTRODUCTION

ALAN GOOD

I'm probably exaggerating when I say my first rejection nearly killed me, but goddamn. It sure felt like it. At least Twitter didn't exist yet.

Part of the problem was I had too high an opinion of myself; I thought I was going to sail straight to the top. It's true, yeah, I was a big idiot. I'd been in two creative writing classes and enjoyed them, did well. People liked my stories. They responded to them in ways they didn't to other people's stories. One guy even refused to give back his copy of a story I wrote called "The Exception." It was an homage to Kafka, probably pretty funny, probably pretty derivative, but I don't remember because I don't have a copy and it seems I deleted it from my hard drive during one of the bouts of depression that ate up my twenties. This guy, I can't remember his name, he typed up his notes and he asked me to sign my story and he kept it. So if you're out there, and you've still got that story—well, it's still not worth anything, just burn it. But scan it first and send it to me. In general, though, while it's okay to be enthusiastic about a young writer, I think maybe asking for their autograph in a writing workshop is a really dangerous idea.

I don't have records from my early days of submitting, don't know if I could stand to look through them if I did; the point is I racked up more rejections and they all hurt, but each one hurt a little less. I eventually got lucky and picked up a couple acceptances, which sustained me through the dry spells. At this point I've endured many hundreds of rejections, nearly ninety just for my first novel. I'm at a point in my career (if you can call it that) as a writer where rejection doesn't hurt anymore, even though it still does.

We called this anthology *Dear Writer* because that's something litmag editors actually say in their rejection emails:

Dear Writer,

Thank you for gracing us with the pleasure of reading your genuinely magnificent story. Reading it truly was a sublime, transformative experience. Sad to say but, unfortunately, it is not the right fit for us at this time.

Best,

The Editors

Nothing irritates me more than the Dear Writer email; of course now, having served as an editor, I understand the utility. Dear Writer may be impersonal, but it's more efficient, and it spares the editor from having to spell people's names right. If you're using Submittable you can get that done for you, but Submittable costs money. We used regular old-fashioned email. Between this book and another anthology we published, I had to send more than a hundred very unpleasant rejection emails, and I addressed each one personally, which meant I did spell one person's name wrong. It was mortifying and required an apologetic follow-up email. But a generic greeting would be more mortifying.

Writers like to complain about their rejections, and I think it's a good practice. There's no need to call out individual editors or publications over a rejection, unless someone has done something highly unethical or cruel, but it's good for the editors on Twitter (okay, most of them are writers, too) to be reminded that there's a genuine, feeling, vulnerable person on the other end of every rejection email. Anyway most of the rejections I've received have been pretty bland, but the most pretentious one I remember went something like "Sad to say, but we cannot accept this." That was one rejection where I felt like I missed a bullet.

Off-topic but I'm just gonna throw this out there: editors, don't call your rejections "declines." They're fucking rejections. Don't try to spin it.

Some writers and editors are full of advice about getting published, this is the best way to write a cover letter, this is what you shouldn't do, this is what you have to do, and honestly who gives a fuck? I don't mean to disparage them, but one thing I learned, I think after my two-hundred-ninety-sixth rejection, is that the way to get published is to just keep going. Keep writing. Keep sending your work out. If it's good, at some point someone will notice it. That's the key. There's just so much good writing, so much bad as well, and it's hard for anyone to notice it, including the editors who are looking for it. Forgive me for quoting my own tweet, but I posted the following from the @MalarkeyBooks account because editing this book showed me it was true: "Hello if 50 editors reject your story that doesn't mean it sucks or that you suck or even that all of those editors suck. The 51st editor might love your shit. Maybe the 87th, I don't know. This isn't an inspirational tweet by the way, it's just science." The criteria to be considered for this anthology was that your story had to have been rejected at least ten times, but few of the stories that made it in were actually rejected ten times. Most were rejected far more frequently than that. And one of them, I'm not making this up, was rejected two hundred times, if you include non-responses as rejections, which you should do. The thing about that story is it's good. It's kind of weird, kind of funny, kind of sad. But it's good. All the stories in this collection are good. I've read them all four or five times now and I still like them and I'm grateful the ten writers whose work we were able to include in this book didn't give up after a few rejections.

Look, bad stories are going to get rejected, but a rejection doesn't tell you anything about the quality of your story because good stories get rejected all the time. Could be it was too long or not long enough or had too many swears or too many adverbs or too many typos or in some ineffable way it just didn't conform to the sensibilities of a certain publication at that time or the editor or intern, depending on where you're querying, didn't even finish reading it.

I lied, okay, none of this is science. Certain stories might never get published. We had to reject a whole bunch of stories in the process of making this book. Some of the stories we didn't like, or they just didn't connect with us. But we also had to reject several stories we did like simply because we didn't have enough money to pay to include them. This is slippery stuff. Your story might get rejected because the journal ran a story on a similar subject in a recent issue, or it might get rejected because it genuinely sucks but the editor doesn't have the heart to say it. The thing to remember is you can't control how an editor's going to react to your story, but, and I'm really annoyed at myself for even saying it like this, you can control how you react to rejections. You know, don't write back and tell the editors they're pieces of shit and don't go on Twitter and say *Blah Blah Blah Literary Journal* is a bunch of fucking tasteless phonies. But also don't quit writing because some editors reject your work. Just keep writing. Just keep querying. Your belief in your work might be delusional, and it might be justified, and the only way to find out, if it's possible to find out, is to just keep going.

Iron and blood

Sarah Evans

I'm standing here in transition, wishing myself somewhere—anywhere—else. Around me is the shove and buzz of people, everyone looking purposeful, and likely some of them I recognize, only the camaraderie from last night is gone. This is competitive, after all.

I strip down to racer-back vest and Lycra shorts, and step into my wetsuit, fitting myself with a second, thicker skin. It feels slimy and cold, smells of rubber and disinfectant. I squeeze my toes into neoprene and my skull into silicone.

I join the huddle on the lakeshore. The others are mostly blokes, mostly younger, all more muscled. I stretch down, fingertips brushing grass. I jump up and down, only it doesn't stop the shiver of morning frost and of anticipation.

The lead competitors line up. Silence falls.

Bang!

They're jumping into the shallows, then plunging forward and I catch the spluttering spray. A gap opens.

I make sure the chip strapped to my wrist registers. Go, go, go!

I hit the shock of ice water. My arms thrash and fail to grip. Bobbing up, I gulp white foam. Wild water is a different medium to chlorine calm and all my training sinks.

Currents pull me back; a crush of bodies blocks my course. Just keep going. And I'm gliding into my rhythm now, gaining warmth, building momentum, breathing every third slow stroke. Keep that heartbeat nice and steady.

2.4 miles. An easy workout in my local pool. Out here it's going to feel ten times farther. Focus, Amy, focus. Keep to that straight-line as best you can.

Three months ago and mostly the online form was straightforward, name, gender and age type thing.

How long have you been training? Two years. (On and off.)

My most important reason for training is: -- -.

Steve came up behind. "I wouldn't mind knowing that," he said, a sneer to his voice, like any answer I might give would just be stupid.

"Well I don't do it to piss you off," I shot back, immediately regretting my tone.

"Why then?"

I train to feel better about myself. That was the best sound bite I could come up with, the answer not boiling straightforwardly down to words. "Aren't there easier ways?" Steve asked.

Easy is hardly the point; since when did easy get you anywhere?

I turn. I'm heading back and there's more space and the pacing feels good.

The end approaches. Kick vigorously: belatedly I remember. Force the blood down into your legs. My knees are already knocking against the stones of the lake bed and I'm hauling myself up to wade back toward the shore. The air smells of watery green.

Everything blurs.

Then clears.

I make sure the chip registers and check my time. Eighty-five minutes, thirty-four seconds. I'm behind my game-plan. I feel emptied out.

The huddle is thinner than before. I'm placed amongst the stragglers, the strugglers, those who might not see it through.

Last night at camp, we formed a shifting community built on shared obsession. All of us dreaming the same dream. We talked previous events, strategies and training routines. My hours of running, cycling, swimming, gym, of fitting training into mornings, evenings, lunchtimes, into weekends and holidays, no longer seemed enough. See! Others do this much harder, I wanted to tell Steve.

"'Guess we're all addicts," someone said, provoking a Mexican wave of knowing smiles.

My name is Amy Davis and I'm an exercise junkie.

Everyone's addicted to something. Fags, booze, illegal highs. Chocolate, McDonald's, Dulcolax. Sex, Prozac, aspirin. As addictions go, surely this is better than the alternatives. Side effects are beneficial, mostly. Try telling Steve that.

I'm back in transition and seek my bag— standout red-orange stripes—and my bike. My Orca wetsuit sticks and peeling it away requires super strength. Come on! A volunteer—dark-haired and skinny—approaches to help and I could kiss him. Shorts and vest are soaked, but they're with me for the ride. I put on socks and fumble with cycling shoes. Seconds are ticking away and my numbed fingers refuse to tighten the helmet. My volunteer can help with that as well. He fixes my competitor number in place, then slathers on coconut-scented factor 50. Come on! His fingers run up my thighs and down into my neckline, but there's zero erotic charge. "We never have sex these days," Steve grumbles. "When you're not off training, you're too knackered or sore."

Check supplies: water, hi-energy gel, extra sodium. Put on sunglasses, gulp down half a water bottle and start steering toward the start.

I'm trembling so hard I can hardly keep my balance. I push forward and down until the cleats in my shoes clip onto the pedals.

Make sure the chip registers. Go, go!

I'm cycling through the crowds and they're cheering me on like I'm Bradley Wiggins. I love you all too! I try to remember the last time Steve said "I love you" without following it with a but.

Swim muscles are slow to toggle down, cycle muscles have yet to ramp up and it's like I'm swimming through air on a metal contraption. I can't do this. 112 miles lie ahead, and that's fine as rides go, nothing too over the top. If it wasn't for the swim. For what comes after.

Focus, Amy, focus.

First stretch is straight and level and my legs are remembering how this goes. I'm huddled into streamline mode. Go for it. Except I mustn't. Keep it steady, keep that heartbeat good and slow.

The gradient tilts. Not harsh, but it's against me. Lactic acid is building in my legs, and too much will burn and slow me down. If I can just reach the top of the incline, it'll be smooth going. If I can just, can just . . .

I switch out from aches and tiredness. I just need to get there.

And here I am.

The top flattens, the gradient flips and my god I've earned this: a short free-sail. I grasp one of my energy tubes. The tear-off top gives all at once, a splurge of yellow gunge over my gloved hand. I suck it off. Quick-release calories, plus caffeine. Synthetic pineapple taste; cake-mix texture.

I'm back to pedaling and nausea presses. Not so fast. Allow blood to direct itself to guts. This complete awareness of self, of body, it's something I've learned and I wonder how I could ever have been so oblivious before.

The sickness eases down. The air is cold and clear in my lungs. Blood pulses in my veins.

I train to feel better about myself. To feel stronger in my body and in my life. For the solitude of a misty evening, the slap of wet pavement beneath my feet, the breeze through my hair like a lover's fingers, the harmony of body, earth, and air. For the fellowship of group training and those moments when it's over and there's the triumph of looking back. For the bliss of blackout sleep. I train for those fly-by instants when I'm outside myself and soaring upwards on the wing. I sense it now, teasing at the edges, that feeling of complete aliveness, like teetering on the edge of orgasm, and you're waiting for the rush, the point of giving in. I tried explaining it to Steve. "Well you may prefer jerking off with your bike," he said. "I don't."

I didn't mean it like that.

This is easy. I'll finish with ease.

I feel a fine mist on my face, look up into a golden spray. The guy ahead is pissing in situ. Thanks! Last night, it was a shared joke. Today, piss in my face is all too vile and I'm landing with a thud back into myself, my everyday self who hurts and who isn't anywhere near as fit as she needs to be. I shift out of the tailwind. My race plan is gone adrift. I am planning to survive.

The slope tips from down to up. My muscles thrum with background pain which lies at the ready to build.

I'm across the line and dismounting like an elephant. I stumble and struggle to remain upright. Everything aches. My bike bounces on the tarmac. A volunteer is there to whisk it away. She smiles; I lack the energy to smile back. I confirm my chip has clocked and check my time. Shit! Double shit! Far too close to the eleven-hour mark. My brain's a blur and the arithmetic to figure out the scale of the problem escapes me. All I know is that I'm behind schedule.

I head for transition. I change into running shoes and strap my hot-pink race belt—fluid and gels—to my waist. Taking a bathroom break, my pee is pungent and dark. My thighs quiver and shake. I head out for the line.

My chip registers. Go, Amy, go!

I'm away, but crawling, up against a brick wall beyond which lies a marathon. Don't think! I've trained for this transition: bike to run, bike to run. Doesn't feel like it.

Transition from drink-addled slob with yo-yo-weight to super-fit: Steve claims he liked my softness and getting sloshed together. It's not just my body that has hardened, but something more basic, he says. He's right. I used to be such a pushover. Fat kid gets bullied at school and walked over in every crap job she ever took. And that's before we start talking the disaster zone of relationships.

I bully myself now and that's different.

Leg muscles are short from pedaling; they need stretching for the run. My body needs to loosen, but it's fist-tight with soreness and exhaustion. Cushioned soles fail to provide a bounce. Exhaustion is too everyday tame to describe the craving to just stop and curl up and die. This is what it must feel like to be a super-centenarian. I'm one hundred and ten years old and attempting to run a marathon. What kind of sick joke is that? What the hell was I thinking? I've worked my way up from beginner's events, but Iron Man is tough as it gets.

Others will already have finished and I seriously hate them. Not for being faster, but for reaching the end. They'll be sky-high on triumph and champagne. Mustn't think. Focus on the here and now, the step-by-step pounding. Each step brings me closer; each step is killing me: one of those will win out eventually.

I find a sort of tempo, but it doesn't flow.

To feel better about myself: remember tapping that out, Amy? So why am I feeling nine-tenths dead?

"Promise me this'll be the last," Steve said and right now I have no argument with that. Never again! God's fury has descended, the plague of locusts, boils, and whatever: they have all arrived as one. Suffering is my lot; it is what I've chosen. If this was easy, everyone would be doing it, but why would anyone even want to? It hurts. It's going to hurt more. I am slammed up against my limits, torturing myself. I possess the means to stop, I mean I can just stop right now, I don't even have to give anything up or betray anyone. I remember the certainty I could do this. The determination that I would finish. But how? Why?

Why, Amy, why?

Should just quit dreaming. Quit aspiring to be something—someone—that I'm not.

"No shame in giving up." Steve's words slither into my mind. Even if I finish, I'll be outside the cutoff and that won't count. Why bother? Why carry on? Give up. Give in. Accept that this was never meant for the likes of you.

Can't go any faster. Can't complete this. Can't. Can't.

And yet I somehow can.

The taunt of failure skulks in every shadowy corner of my mind, one more letdown ready to be added to my list.

I failed to carry a baby to term. My fertility is screwed, ovaries packing in too soon. I fail to see the point of sex just now.

I train so that I will finish things, so that just once I won't fall short. Pain is with me every step, but I'm beyond any possibility of stopping.

A lifetime later and I glimpse the Timex clock, held up high. I'm into the final straight. My vision's blurred, can't make out the digits, all I can do is continue my limp-limp-drag toward the finish. Seconds are ticking on. A few either way makes no difference; it makes all the difference. I've nothing left for a final spurt.

Enough of the crowd remains to put up a decent cheer, encouraging me along, and I'm in love with each and every one of them. Come on, come on! Fists are raised and one of them is mine. I'm at the line. Over it. I check my chip has registered and collapse in a heap. I taste grit. I am never getting up. One of the volunteers comes over to help me onto my feet and tidy me out of the way.

"Congratulations," he says. "You did it."

I did it.

I'm an Iron Woman, a woman made of iron. I feel the pulse. My high rises way above the feeling of total fucked-up-ness.

Swim 2.4 miles. Bike 112 miles. Run 26.2 miles. Brag for the rest of your life! And I intend to.

Total time: sixteen hours, fifty-seven-minutes, twenty-three seconds. Cutoff: seventeen hours. I go round idiotically thanking everyone. Volunteers. Spectators. Competitors.

I train to fill the empty spaces. To quieten the voices in my head. I train because I need to, like I need to breathe. I inhale my sour-smell body and feel my heartbeat settle and every inch of me throbs and I'm every inch alive.

I take my running shoes off to give my blistered feet some air. I ought to get checked out by the medics. Ought to find a bath of ice. Cold will be agony; it'll pay off in recovery time.

Then I see. A figure out of context walks toward me. "Don't expect me to come watch," he'd said.

But Steve is here and grinning like he's pleased for me and proud of me. I stagger forward and his arms wrap me close, pressing my sweat-drenched vest to my back. I hear his breath in my ear. "Well done, you! You've done fabulously well. Iron woman."

I am not an iron woman; I am made of flesh and blood. Prick me and I bleed all too messily. I'm still that fat and bullied child, the bulimic teenager, the woman who drank way too much and whose screwed-up body couldn't handle carrying a child.

I need Steve's warmth and softness, holding me close. I need the burrowed comfort of his slumbering form through unending sleepless hours. Need his laughter and his solid reassurance, his encouragement and his love. But it isn't enough.

"I need to do this," I say.

He pulls me closer. "I know, I know."

My muscles scream, but I hold on tighter.

I train to feel better about myself. To conquer pain and fear and loss. I train because being alive is hard; it hurts. But it's better than the alternative, and since when did easy get you anywhere?

AND THEN IT WAS OVER

YOUSEF ALLOUZI

T he sun shone brightly through the second-story window, and its warmth spilled over his face and hands. His desk shielded the lower half of his body from the heat, but he didn't seem to notice. He sat in silence, staring out at the world below. He used to open the window, back when a computer and printer occupied the desk. Both sat in the bottom of his closet gathering a thick layer of dust. He remembered how he would smell the bread from the sandwich shop down the street. The flowers when they bloomed in spring. Rain, the earth, the smell of a barbecue somewhere in the neighborhood. Lance watched a cloud of tiny dust particles floating in the sunshine.

Most of the time, all he felt was pain. But on some mornings, when the medicine was just right, he could still sit with only slight discomfort and find himself thinking about what his life had once been like. He rubbed his hand across the top of the empty desk. He loved the feeling of heat and then cool that the areas of sunlight and then shade provided. The room was otherwise empty. He had rid himself of most of his possessions. His desk, however, was one thing he could never part with. He looked down at the bottom drawer and sat staring at its handle. He reached out to open it, but stopped once he touched metal. Then he slowly leaned back in his chair, until his hand fell from the handle down to his knee. He let his gaze move slowly from the drawer back up the desk to the window, pausing at the scratches and pen marks that he found. He had paid ten bucks for it at a garage sale. It was bulky and heavy. Now that he thought about it, it was because of the scratches and pen marks that he bought it. Scars were something that they both had in common.

From the perch of his window, Lance watched the trees move with the wind. He had fallen in love with Portland. He had Heather to thank, although he didn't like to admit it. He had moved from Albuquerque because of her. Cars and kids scurried to work and school below him. A group of middle-aged women were jogging down the street, bundled in jackets and sweatshirts. White puffs of air seemingly froze behind them. He watched the small clouds slowly melt into the chilly morning. He recalled that he used to go for walks and before that runs.

Lance knew the daily rituals of the neighborhood. School bus at seven-thirty. The usual five kids were waiting patiently at the corner, including the little fat kid who picked on the others. Today, the bus was late. Lance felt his stomach growl, but he was not hungry. He watched the children stand idly, as the fat kid threw rocks across the street. Eventually, some parents came and took a few of the kids. He noted that the fat kid's parents did not come. Lance began to wonder about what might have happened to the bus. Finally, when it did arrive, it was not the usual yellow school district bus he was accustomed to seeing. Instead, he watched a poorly painted flat-white bus pull up awkwardly beside the curb. Mechanical problems, he resumed his assessment, but before he could fully develop his thoughts, he was suddenly jarred by a vague memory. A white bus from his youth.

***

"Its 6 a.m." His mother's hand shook him from sleep. "Get up. You are going to church," she said. He quietly dressed, half asleep, and stum-

bled from the back of the trailer into the kitch-
en. Instant oatmeal was in the cupboard, Lance
heard his mother say. He ate in silence. "Now
brush your teeth," she ordered. "The bus will
be here soon." He got up and went to the bathroom, his tired footsteps echoing down the
small, dark panel hallway. As he brushed his
teeth, Rusty came into the bathroom behind
him, slicking back his thin brown hair and
smoking a cigarette. He stood in his underwear,
now staring at Lance in the mirror through
bloodshot eyes. "You woke me up," Rusty said
coldly as smoke poured from his mouth. Lance
froze, staring back at Rusty's twisted nose in
the bathroom mirror. "You look like a hippie,"
Rusty said. He took the hairbrush off the counter and began to run it forcefully through
Lance's hair. "I just want some sleep, is that too
much to ask?" Rusty said calmly, the cigarette
now bouncing up and down in response to his
moving lips. Lance remained still despite the
toothpaste dripping onto his shirt. He felt the
force of the brush increasing on his scalp.
"Why can't you be quiet?" Rusty continued,
just above a whisper. Lance remained silent.
"Your nappy-ass hair just won't stay where I
put it." Rusty's Southern accent came on angrily. The tension suddenly broke, and Rusty
slapped Lance on the back of the head with the

hard plastic brush. It made Lance's vision spin, and he felt a strong pain in the back of his head. Lance tried to reach back and place his hand over his head, but before he could Rusty slapped him again. Then he forcefully threw the hairbrush onto the counter. Rusty watched as it crashed onto the floor. Rusty balled his fist and Lance cowered. "Get the fuck outta here and learn to be quiet," Rusty said through clenched teeth. Lance ran outside to wait for the white church van. With tears in his eyes, he heard the door lock behind him.

***

There were no longer any children on the street corner when Lance became aware again. He felt anger just below the skin. The air in the room felt hot and stale and smelled like disinfectant. The flood of memories from his childhood made it hard for him to breathe. He felt his chest rise and fall and Lance struggled to control his breathing and calm himself down. He felt his fists clench and his jaw set. He rocked slightly in the chair. "Breathe you fuck," he said to himself repeatedly as the tide of emotion crashed through his body. "C'mon you pussy," he thought, as his vision became blurry. He blinked repeatedly to wick away the tears.

After a time, he felt the emotion recede as his clenched fists and heavy breathing slowly returned to normal. The memories, however, ran wild through his mind and Lance had no choice but to succumb.

**

The high school security guard grabbed him by his jacket and pulled him off the bloody heap he had been uncontrollably punching. He smiled violently as he was hauled to the principal's office. Euphoria swept over his body. He felt an emptying out, like all that had been inside of him had been purged. He sat outside the principal's office. "Lance Sellers," the principal finally called from his desk. Lance got up and went inside. He sat down across from the principal, who did not look up from the paper he held in his hand. "This has become a recurring problem with you. Do you have an explanation?" Lance sat silent. The principal shook his head. "You've been warned too many times before," he heard the principal say. "I'm suspending you from school for a week. We will reassess your fit for the school when you come back." The principal was now looking at Lance directly. Lance sat staring back. He didn't care about being suspended. He rarely even came to class. "Do you have anything you want to add?" Lance continued his silence. "Your mother is on her way to pick you up," the principal finally said. Lance sat expressionless; he hadn't been home in over a week. "You can wait outside my office." The principal pointed through the door to the chair that Lance had previously occupied. Lance rose to his feet, walked out of the office, and sat.

He sat in silence inside the van, as his mother drove him home. "Rusty is waiting for you," he thought she said. Lance felt like he was outside of his body. He watched his mom from this new perspective. She looked old and scared, her face more wrinkled than he remembered, her hands creased. She seemed as if she was rotting from the inside out. He thought that he should say something, but he couldn't find the words. He struggled for sympathy. Instead, he found only indifference.

The inside of the house smelled familiar to Lance. It immediately made his skin crawl. He first saw Rusty in the kitchen, leaning on the oven, chewing loudly on a fried bologna sandwich. He stared at Lance intensely. Lance quickly looked away, choosing to stare at the bologna rinds, mustard bottle, and breadcrumbs on the counter. The exhaust fan above muted the still-sizzling cast-iron skillet on the stove. Lance began watching the small pieces of bologna popping and frying inside the pan. Then, from the corner of his eye, he saw the belt Rusty was holding. This particular belt was worse than the sticks, fists, and metal pipes he would sometimes use. Raised metal letters ran across it, R-U-S-T-Y. This was followed by raised metal eagle medallions, somehow attached, which ran on either side of his name around to the buckle. Lance was immediately struck with an overwhelming fear. He had been kept home from school for a week the last time Rusty had used it. Lance slowly backed away. As he turned to bolt for the door, he felt the belt slap across his back and a fire ignite across his skin. He reached out for the doorknob, but Rusty had already grabbed him by his shirt. He quickly pinned Lance against the door. "Tell me you're sorry," Rusty said calmly but forcefully. Lance remained silent. "I said tell me you're sorry," Rusty repeated, this time a bit louder. Again, Lance did not respond. "Goddamnit, you fucking piece of shit," Rusty exploded. He punched Lance in the stomach. Lance thought he might throw up as he went down on one knee. Rusty followed with the belt, striking Lance repeatedly. "Tell me you are sorry!" Rusty screamed. He continued to strike Lance violently until the muscles in his arm ached. Then he kneeled down and leveled himself with Lance, who was now lying on his stomach on the floor. "Listen to me," Rusty whispered. "I'm only going to say this one more time. Tell me you are sorry." Lance remained defiant. Rusty put his knee on the back of Lance's neck and then shifted his weight. Lance felt pressure in his head and a sharp pain in his neck. He cringed in silence. Not receiving a response, Rusty beared down with even more force. Lance began to feel that his neck would snap. "I'm sorry," Lance finally whispered. "Say it where I can hear it!" Rusty boomed. "I'm sorry!" Lance screamed as tears flowed down across his nose and onto the floor. Rusty paused, then slowly began to smile. He stood up to relieve the pressure on Lance's neck. He adjusted his shirt and used his hand to slick back his hair. "Yes, you are," he finally said, as he wrapped the belt back through his pants loops.

That night, Lance left his mother's house for good. He had scraped together enough money to buy a bus ticket to Albuquerque, where an aunt he liked lived. He wondered if his mother and Lance would even notice he was gone. On the bus, Lance tried not to move too much. If he leaned the wrong way, he felt pain across his back and neck. A deep anger welled up inside of him. He felt ashamed and insecure. As he sat awkwardly, looking at his own reflection in the window, he resolved to never allow himself to feel this way again.

***

Lance once again found himself staring at the bottom drawer of his desk. He pushed aside his thoughts and glanced over at the alarm clock beside his bed. Eleven-thirty. The day was moving faster than usual. He imagined himself throwing the alarm clock out the window and then smashing it with a hammer. He had spent his whole damn life chained to a clock. Irritated, he turned his attention back toward the window. The sandwich shop on the corner was already packed. A stream of businesspeople darted about almost robotically. They rushed in and rushed out. Some ordered and ate at the tables by the big bay window. But even these radicals did so with purpose and speed. There was little time for talk. Lance struggled to see in detail. His vision had deteriorated significantly. He was able to make out two college-aged kids walking hand in hand. They struck a contrast from the robots in suits and skirts ordering sandwiches. They walked without a stated purpose. They seemed not to notice that they were not as important. They sat at the tables by the big bay window. They talked. They laughed. They stayed for over an hour. Lance hoped that they would somehow escape their fate. That they could keep laughing and talking forever. Lance had never learned how to talk.

A sudden knock on the door broke him from his thoughts. He didn't get up to open it, as the sound of the key turning in the lock told him that his son, Michael, had finally come. "You're early," Lance barked. Michael smiled. "I know. Good to see you, too." He paused. "Where's your nurse?" Lance rolled his eyes. "No nurses. No volunteers. None of that shit." He lightly waved his index finger back and forth. Michael shook his head and then shrugged his shoulders. "Okay, Dad." Every day for the past few years, since Lance had first been diagnosed with cancer, Michael had taken care of his father. He brought him groceries when he needed them, took him to the doctor, stayed at the hospital when it got too bad, and had suffered through the rounds of chemotherapy and overall significant decline in his father's health. The doctor had originally told Lance that he had only two months to live. Yet here he was, three years later, still fighting. Michael held a bottle of twenty-one-year-old Glenlivet Archive Scotch, a Cuban cigar, and a sealed envelope. "I brought everything you asked for." "I didn't ask for an envelope," Lance sniped. "It's from Mom," Michael followed. "She wants to try and patch things up. She sent this for you." Lance tried not to look surprised. "Put the Scotch on the table," he said softly. "Keep the cigar, and grab the cutter. I think we're going to go for a walk." Michael looked skeptical. "Are you sure you're up for it? What about this letter from mom?" Lance didn't respond. Michael understood that his father had already made up his mind. He couldn't help but chuckle at his father's stubbornness. He put the letter on the table as tears welled up in his eyes. He fought hard to keep them from running down his face. He felt just like a child again. He still wanted to be tough and strong like his father. "The wife and kids didn't want to come?" Lance interrupted. "Looks like it's just you and me, Dad."

Michael carefully helped his father into a heavy jacket. He gently placed gloves on his father's hands and a beanie on his head. "Help me out of this chair," Lance said gently. It pained Michael to feel his father so fragile, as he slowly pulled him up. He remembered how strong his father had been in his youth. He had been all but bedridden for nearly six months. Michael helped his father through the door. The next challenge was the stairs. For reasons that were not entirely clear, Lance had demanded to live on the second floor. No doctor, nurse, or family member could convince him otherwise. Even when he became confined to the room, he refused to be moved. Michael supposed it had something to do with his father's love for the window but a lot more to do with his pride. Michael suggested carrying his father down to the bottom. "You'd like that, wouldn't you," Lance said. "To carry your old man down the stairs." Lance smiled at the thought. "Maybe I could just ride on your shoulders." They both laughed. The more they laughed the funnier it became. Suddenly, Lance's laugh became wheezing and coughing, wheezing and coughing some more. "Dad," Michael said, alarmed. "I'm okay, son." Michael smiled. "You know," he said as he carefully lifted his father, "I think I *will* carry you." This time, Lance didn't object.

At the bottom of the steps, Michael gently set his father on the ground. He could tell he was in pain. Lance did his best to conceal it. He knew how to deal with it. It had been a part of his life for as long as he could remember. Slowly, step by step, they walked together from the staircase enclosure to the sidewalk. "The bench at the end of the block," Lance wheezed. "Let's sit there awhile." Michael knew it was pointless to argue.

As they walked arm in arm, Lance closed his eyes and took a deep breath. The cold air filled his lungs. He could smell the fresh bread from down the street. "This is what I've missed," he said. Carefully, they made their way to the bench. Lance looked up at his window, now facing down on him. He realized what a narrow view he had from his room. He felt the rush of the wind of the passing cars. A woman with too much perfume dashed hurriedly by. He took in the sights, sounds, and smells as if he had never experienced them before. After a few minutes of wheezing had passed, he turned to Michael. "I want my cigar." Michael fished the cigar from his jacket pocket and the cutter as well. "Seeing that letter you brought from your mother got me to thinking," Lance started, as Michael clipped the cigar end for his father, "that you and I haven't really talked all that much." Michael understood but played coy. "What do you mean?" "I mean I haven't ever been all that open with you," Lance uncomfortably went on. "I guess what I'm trying to say is that there is something you should know about your mother and me." Michael hesitated for a moment but decided to keep quiet. "Your mother . . . ." Lance paused. "Heather is a good person, Michael. You should try to work things out with her. Life is a funny thing. Sometimes things happen that you don't intend." "But I don't know that she does," Michael interrupted. Lance held the cigar in his lips while Michael struck the lighter in his cupped hands. Lance bent down and placed the cigar over the flame as large puffs of smoke now poured out of his mouth. He coughed deeply. "I'm not the best talker, son. I know that." Lance paused and drew another large drag off the cigar. "But I think you should know how everything happened. It's probably something I should have told you a long time ago."

***

Heather moved with a grace Lance had never seen before. He liked how her hair was straight and simple. She was beautiful without makeup. For once in his life, things were easy and carefree. She loved to hear him talk about a variety of topics, and he liked how she stuck to routines and challenged something inside of him. She understood something familiar about him, although they never would talk about it. He took the job in Oregon because she had urged him for a fresh start. The lumber mill outside of Portland didn't pay much, but he managed to save for a year straight. He bought the ring with all he had.

The Oregon Zoo was not very busy in April and looking at the lions, monkeys, and giraffes felt surreal. Every minute or two, he would feel inside his pocket to make sure the ring was still there. When they finally got to the penguin section, he pulled her close and kissed her gently. She returned his embrace. "I love penguins," he said, "because they mate for life." She smiled. "You know that because I told you that." "No," he said, brushing this obvious truth aside and dropping to one knee. "I know that because I want you to be my penguin. Will you marry me?" Streams of tears ran down her face, as she pulled him up from his knee. "Yes," she whispered. As they kissed again, the crowd of people that had gathered around them began to clap.

***

Michael looked over at his father. Lance was slowly puffing on his cigar, plumes of smoke rising into the air. He was deep in thought. He was back with Heather. "So what happened?" Michael finally found the courage to say. "Why did you guys split up?" Lance did not respond. He just kept at the cigar. Michael noticed that the gentle nature of his father had vanished. This, Michael was sure, was why his father had never remarried. In fact, he had never seen his father date anyone for as long as he could remember. Michael thought he had pushed too far. "I'm sorry I asked, Dad," he said in a low tone. Lance blinked but did not move. Then, he looked over at Michael and tried to form some words. "Let's get you home," Michael interjected. He stood up to help his father, but Lance began to speak, slow and distant at first.

***

The Christmas lights Lance had put up cast a wonderful glow off the snow on the ground. More glided down thick and quiet. He stopped in front of the house. He had never seen it from this angle before, and he almost determined that it wasn't his. The lighted "Merry Christmas" sign he had hung reassured him that he was home. He loved this time of year. Walking toward his front door he could hear "Rockin' Around the Christmas Tree" playing in the neighbor's house, and he was overcome by a strange nostalgia from his youth. He had managed to get off early from the lumber mill and was anxious to get home to Heather and Michael. The smell of the pines that surrounded the cul-de-sac hung dense in the air. The snow crunched under his feet, and the bitter cold stung his ears and nose. Snow, falling even harder now, almost drowned the red from the dozen roses he clutched. Reaching the door, he was surprised to find it unlocked. From the foyer, he could see that all the furniture was missing from the living room. He stood puzzled, then walked quickly into their bedroom. He turned on the light and saw the portion of the closet where the door was still open, the bright white paint the only thing inside. Lance found that every room in the house was the same. Only his clothes and a note folded in half on the kitchen counter remained. The top of it read, "Lance." Overwhelmed and confused, he collapsed in the middle of his now-empty living room and tried to gather his thoughts.

***

Lance's voice trailed off. Michael returned to the uncomfortable silence. After a long while, Lance finally spoke again: "I looked every-where for you guys. I thought I was going crazy. A few weeks later, your mom called me out of the blue and asked me if I wanted to take care of you. I left that day for Albuquerque. I picked you up at your grandma's house and that's how we got to where we are today. I'm sorry I haven't ever really explained it to you." Lance took another puff on his cigar. "What happened between your mother and me, that was a long time ago. We were different people then. It took me a long time to realize that it wasn't only her fault." Lance turned and looked at Michael. "Don't be like me. See if you can work it out with her." Lance put the cigar out and noticed that his hand was shaking. Looking back at Michael, he nodded toward his window. "I'm ready to go home."

They walked in silence back to the stairs. Carrying his father again, Michael thought about how his father would carry him when he was a child. Michael began to feel dizzy as he walked back through the door of the apartment, but was careful not to let his father scrape against the frame. As he carefully set his father back into his chair, he hesitated a moment, letting the warmth and smell of his father linger for a bit longer. He slowly wrapped his arms around him. He couldn't remember the last time he had hugged his father. He felt a heavy pressure on his chest and when his father's arms returned his embrace, the tears burst from inside of him. He held his father and cried. He cried for time. He cried for love. He cried for his father.

As the last bits of sunlight shone in through the window, Lance and Michael now sat quiet. When the first few stars became visible, Lance broke the calm. "Have a glass of Scotch with your old man." Michael brought over the bottle of Glenlivet and two whisky glasses. He opened the bottle and poured two drinks. Lance lifted his glass in the air. "To life," he pronounced. "To life," Michael's voice cracked. Lance took a sip and let the buttery single malt glide over his tongue. "I have so much I want to tell you, son," Lance said quietly. "But I just don't know how." The moonlight now shone in through the window and illuminated the desk. The rest of the room remained black. Lance stared out of the window, and Michael could just see tears reflecting in the light as they ran down his cheeks. He took a long drink of his whisky to help calm his growing anxiety. Mustering his strength, Lance suddenly reached down and pulled open the bottom drawer of his desk. He stared for a moment at the bottle of Nembutal and then took it out of the drawer and set it beside the bottle of whisky. "Dad, please," Michael whispered in a soft tone. "Don't do it. Let's keep fighting. I can't be here without you." Tears were streaming down his face. "Michael," Lance began, "I've spent my whole life fighting. I'm tired. You were always meant to be here without me. My job was to get you here, to this point." Michael began to argue with his father, but Lance did not hesitate. He opened the Nembutal and after taking a deep breath drank the entire bottle without pause. He immediately chased it with the remainder of his Scotch. "I love you, Michael," Lance whispered, as Michael now sobbed uncontrollably. "Help me to lay down."

Michael lay his father's body in bed, then laid down beside him, as he had done when he was a child. Lance took his hand. "I asked you to come today because there was nobody in this world I would rather be with," he whispered, eye to eye with Michael. "I'm sorry, I haven't asked you a very easy thing." Lance mustered a sleepy smile. "But I'm so proud of you son. I love you so much." Michael watched his father's eyes growing heavier with every blink. "I love you too, Dad. I'm so sorry." Lance held his smile and locked eyes with his son. Michael could feel his father's grip slowly becoming weaker and for the first time he understood what it meant to be alone in the world. Through teary eyes, Michael gently turned his father's body so he could see out of his window. Lance tried to thank Michael, but struggled with the words. He looked out above the trees at the flickering lights in the night sky. Then he moved through the moonlight down past the bench, through the bus stop, and ever faster into the growing blackness that engulfed him.

THE OURRIHN:

THE FIRST ALIEN REFUGEES ON EARTH

KAREN THROWER

I was fifteen when the massive, silver ship landed in the isolated forests of Russia. I remember everyone being curious and scared. It was the first time a spacecraft wasn't just a blurry thing in the background of a shaky video. Rumors flew around the internet for weeks about the ship. Where was it was from, who was in there, etc. Was this an ambassador trip and we were going to get a new ally? Or was this the first step in an invasion and we were about to be enslaved? We waited, day after day, week after week, for something to emerge from the ship, but no one exited. The fear was slowly replaced with caution when nothing happened after a month. Whoever was in the ship made no move, hostile or otherwise. They simply showed up, landed, and waited.

It was breaking news worldwide when, after a month of nothing, something was finally happening. I was in history class when the principal came over the speaker and told the teachers to turn on the news. No one spoke as we watched a big door open on the side of the ship and saw them for the first time. I remember my jaw dropping at the sight. The adults were tall, about seven feet and gorgeously lithe. They wore no clothing but didn't appear to have the usual defining characteristics of either sex that one might cover up. They were smooth from their bald heads to their feet. But their skin was dazzling. It was sparkling silver, but never blinded us with its millions of flickering lights. We watched smaller ones, who we assumed were children, run from the ship and immediately roll in the grass. I remember the whole class chuckling at the sweet sight. The children were four feet tall and their skin seemed more pearlescent than silver. Their eyes were almond-shaped, huge and black. Simply put, the aliens were beautiful.

We watched the taller ones walk down the ramp to the children. Their movements were slow and graceful. We watched as the adults wiggled their feet back and forth through the thick, emerald meadow their ship landed on. Their once-hidden mouths broke out into smiles that put hope in our hearts that they were peaceful. Now we had seen them, we wondered what they would sound like? Would we be able to understand them?

I remember Brad tapping my shoulder. "Hey Hannah, cute huh?" I rolled my eyes at him and turned back to the screen. One of the aliens walked forward and motioned for one of the reporters to come and meet them. All the cameras turned to them as they walked toward the alien. The reporter was a woman named Grace Bailey, and she worked for the BBC. She was followed by her producer and a single cameraman. She stopped in front of the alien and offered her hand. We were surprised to see the alien give it a shake, like it had been doing it for years. Everyone had been tweeting and using social media to suggest what the first thing we say to them should be. Grace stumbled a bit when she spoke, but no one blamed her. It must have been nerve-wracking, being the first human to speak with an alien.

"Wel-uh, um, are—" She cleared her throat. "Welcome, my name is Grace," she finally said.

The alien bowed its head. "Thank you, Grace." It slowly stood straight, the smile staying on their face as it spoke. "My name is Till, and this is my family," it said as it motioned back to the ramp where a dozen others of varying heights stood. I heard a faint gasp as my class listened to Till speak. It was something we'd never forget. Till's voice was as beautiful as they were. Soft and eloquent, Till's accent sounded slightly British but nowhere near as proper as the Queen. We were enthralled and wanted to hear more. I wondered if my teacher wished she were an alien, so we'd pay that much attention to her.

We couldn't tell if Till was male or female, but at the time I don't think we cared. We just wanted to listen to them speak. For hours, the interview was broadcast as breaking news. Not even the most hardcore viewer of *The Price is Right* complained about missing their regular show that day.

"Does your species have a name?" Grace asked.

Till nodded gently. "On our home planet of Aslion, we are known as 'Rihn,'" Till said. "We are explorers, mapping the galaxy." We watched as Till waved its hand and a map made of light appeared in the air. "This is what we have so far." It was massive and showed an impressive number of planets, yet we knew it was only a small piece of the universe. Till pointed out where other species lived in the Milky Way. It was quite sobering, and probably a little ego-hitting to some, to learn we weren't the only ones in the galaxy. "We came upon your planet a year ago and have been observing and learning your customs and languages. So far, we have perfected twenty of your languages. More importantly, we wanted out first meeting to be as calm as possible."

Grace smiled. "I think we're doing rather well."

Till bowed its head. "As do I," it said as one of the smaller aliens hugged its legs. Everyone wanted to know what their purpose was on Earth, and Till promised they had no interest in conquering our planet. They were also willing to share technology with us and strengthen our non-existent planetary defenses. According to Till, they were taken aback when they learned we had none and felt it was their duty to help us create one.

After two hours of camera-click-filled conversation, Till suggested they walk away from the circus of reporters into the lovely field before them. It was filled with soft, tall grass and white flowers. It took the security guards a bit to make a hole in the reporters; nobody wanted to move.

"I wonder what they feel like?" a boy in my class whose named I have forgotten wondered aloud.

"I bet they're soft," my friend Amanda said.

"They look more silky than soft, if that makes sense," I said. The teacher shushed us as little giggles from the alien children filled our ears. We watched the children run through the tall flowers, their giggles like music. I like to think at this moment the entire world was captivated and at peace. At least it was in our little classroom. I wish it had lasted longer. I don't even remember what Grace was asking but I'll never forget watching Till lean down to smell that flower. The camera was pushed in close as we watched Till's large eyes close as it gave a big sniff. A smile spread on their face when a bee flew up from the flowers.

Till gasped and quickly stood straight and backed away from it. "Are there many bees in this field?" Till asked.

"Most likely. It is spring," Grace had said.

"Well that's one thing we have in common with them, we're afraid of bees!" Mike had teased. Till turned to the children and said something in what we assumed was their native language. It was lyrical and complicated. The children gasped and started running for the ship.

"Is something wrong?" Grace asked. We all leaned out of our desks to get a better look. Was it another alien coming to kill them? Was someone running at them with a gun? Why were they scared? It worried us. We didn't want to see them hurt.

"We have studied little of your fauna, pre-ferring to focus on humans and your behavior. When we discovered your bees, their stinger became a concern to us," Till said.

"Oh. Well it might hurt a little but if you're not allergic it's nothing to be afraid of."

Everyone wanted Grace to succeed in calm-ing Till, no one wanted them to be afraid. Till walked after the children and the camera crew followed.

"It is not us we are concerned for," Till said. "We are unsure of how our bodies will react in your atmosphere and—" Till gasped and held its hand close to its face. The camera zoomed in and we saw a bee sitting on Till's hand, the stinger buried in that sparkling, silver skin.

"Oh shit, that little asshole stung her!" Mike yelled out. I'm sure the teacher would have scolded him for the language, except what hap-pened next shocked us all into silence.

"Please know," Till said, "we mean you no harm." Till looked at the camera then poofed into a large cloud of gray mist. Everyone gasped, and we could hear the Rihn children in the background screaming. It was frightening and heartbreaking. The main feed changed to a camera by the ship and the camera with Grace was put into a small box at the bottom of the screen, so we could watch both.

"What the hell was that?" I whispered. Our teacher shook her head in disbelief and I swear I saw a tear roll down her cheek.

We watched as the mist spread a good twenty meters from where Grace and her crew had been standing. In the smaller screen we could no longer see Grace or her producer; they had been obscured by the mist. But they had left Grace's microphone open, and we could hear her and her co-workers choking and coughing inside the mist. Finally, a gust of wind blew some of the mist away and I knew there was a collective gasp around the world as we saw them.

Grace and her producer were lying on the ground, convulsing violently. A few girls in class screamed and covered their eyes. I didn't blame them. Their skin had turned purple and they seemed to be decaying at an accelerated rate. Their purple skin became wrinkly before our eyes and their bodies seemed to shrink. The camera fell to the ground and all we saw was a sneaker, the toe pointing up. It didn't take long before the sneaker was too big for the shrunken foot inside and it fell to its side. Why the station kept it on the air I'll never know. Perhaps they were just as shocked as we were, and it never occurred to them to cut the feed.

It seemed to take forever before the station finally dissolved the little box off screen and we were left with a shot from a camera by the ship. Another tall Rihn was ushering the children inside the ship, yelling at them in their native language. Cameras surrounded the ramp, reporters shouted questions, asking what happened to Till but the alien didn't answer. I had a feeling the Rihn was overwhelmed by the sudden loss of their family member. Its head looked back and forth between the cameras for a moment before it ducked back into the ship after the young ones. The ramp closed, and we were left without answers.

School was dismissed and we all ran home. For weeks it was all anyone talked about, those poor aliens, were they going to leave now? Were they going to attack? All we could do was wait and see.

The Rihn didn't leave the planet, nor did they explain why Till turned into such a dangerous gas. They stayed sequestered in their ship, offering no explanations. It took two days for the mist that was once Till to disperse. The Russian army went in to retrieve the bodies, and even though the air tests confirmed it was clear of contaminants, they wore protective gear as a precaution. About ten people walked into the area wearing yellow hazmat suits. One was testing the air constantly for contaminants with a device but never told the other to leave. Everyone around the world watched as they gently picked up the bodies and put them on the three gurneys. I was grateful they didn't crumble into nothing when the men touched them. They seemed like normal three-day old corpses, except for the purple skin and exsanguinated look they had.

Since what happened to Grace and her co-workers was broadcast over the globe, the United Nations knew they had to keep everyone informed about the autopsies. There was no covering this up, no skipping questions. We needed to know what exactly happened. Every day for weeks our classes would be interrupted by more news reports. The doctors would hold news conferences and let the world know of the littlest things they had found about the bodies. The first thing they reported was that the bodies had been desiccated. As if every bit of water had been siphoned out of their cells. They also found something like endothall in their systems. Except it was made of three salts instead of the usual two that is normally found on Earth. They also found unbelievable amounts of silver nitrate. The doctors said this was the reason for their skin turning purple, causing something called argyria. Normally in small amounts silver nitrate isn't harmful, but at the levels they were exposed to, the change to their skin happened in seconds.

In our chemistry classes we started studying endothall and silver nitrate. Our teachers wanted us to be familiar with these chemicals and I agreed. If we understood these chemicals, we might be able to keep them from harming us, even accidentally. I dove into my studies and won a science fair on my theory that Till's body evaporated like it did due to overacting antibodies combined with the amount of water in the venom of a bee. I won a scholarship, which was great, but I still wished my prize was to meet one of the Rihn. But as they hadn't opened up their ship, it was unlikely. We still held out hope that they would one day open their craft up to us.

For months, we beseeched the Rihn to come out of their ship. We told them that what happened was clearly an accident and we wouldn't pursue any kind of legal or military action against them. But our pleas went unheard. We wondered why they didn't leave? Did they want to wait and see if we'd attack or could they even leave? We offered what help we had, but we heard nothing.

Six months later the ramp finally opened. Like before, the teachers turned on the televisions, so we could watch this momentous occasion. We watched another tall Rihn walk down the ramp. The same graceful movement that Till had. There were more reporters now than when we had first spoke with them. Thankfully they were a bit more subdued. The reporters waited quietly for the Rihn to come to them, as they stood, holding their microphones out. They wanted to catch every word this Rihn said. It walked a few feet away from the ship and seemed to look over the sea of people in front of it.

"We are extremely saddened by the loss of Till, as well as your people." Its voice was just as beautiful as Till's had been. There was a difference in it though, a little deeper than Till's, and I couldn't help but wonder if this one was male. "We have heard your words, that it was an accident and you do not blame us. We also do not blame you for the actions of your native fauna. We understand that bees are essential to your life on this planet and will not eradicate it simply for our sake." Some of the reporters looked at each other, a little shocked that the Rihn had even considered killing the bees.

"Could they do that?" Mike asked.

"They're aliens, of course they could," Amanda said. I had no doubt in my mind they could if they set their minds to it.

The Rihn representative folded its hands in front of its body and lowered its head as it continued. "Till was correct when she said we did little study on your native flora and fauna. We realize now that was a mistake." It raised its head and stared into the cameras. "Had we known what would happen to our bodies on your planet, we would have prepared better. On our planet, our bodies simply dissolve and because we are able to breathe your air, we hoped they would do the same here. But we were wrong, and it is clear our bodies seem to react differently to the mixture of oxygen and water on this planet. We will not make such a mistake or assumption again." It waited a few beats, letting this new information sink in. "My name is Jesk'ck, Till was my mate. When she said we were explorers, she was referring to our family. Our home world is ruled in a, to use one of your words, totalitarian way. We left to find a more tolerant planet. One where we could live in peace. This is the first planet we have found that, despite a few natural obstacles, offers a safe life. One where we can exchange ideas and technology away from the home world."

There was a soft gasp through the reporters as he continued to speak. I remember smiling and looking back at my classmates, excited at having the Rihn live on Earth. Most of us were smiling, but I could see some of them were afraid. "When we first landed, we wanted your permission to build a life here. Not only for my family but for those of us on our home world that wish to escape the brutality of our leaders. The pacifists, to use another of your words. After the accident with the tiny, flying fauna, we thought that might not be possible. But your words of sympathy and understanding have given us hope. Hope that we still might accomplish this. What say you, Humans of Earth. May our people settle here? May we Rihn also call Earth home?" He gave the reporters a bow, then walked back into the ship.

I sat back and sighed. "Wow." Chatter spread through the classroom but all I could think was I might actually get to meet one. They were going to live on Earth, I just knew it.

For weeks, the United Nations discussed the possible repercussions to having an alien species making Earth its home. We watched the sessions with baited breath, waiting for a result. The good, the bad, and the impossible were discussed and, in the end, they invited these pacifist Rihn to live with us on Earth. It was a momentous occasion. It was the first time our planet gave sanctuary. The first time an alien species wanted us to help them. It was unprecedented and celebrated around the world. According to Jesk'ck, there were almost a thousand Rihn that wanted asylum on Earth. They said they would live anywhere we would have them, they could survive in high heat or no heat.

Considering we saw the repercussions of what bees did to them, the United Nations gave them free reign in Antarctica. No bees and lots of soft snow. Jesk'ck seemed happy when he learned this. He said they didn't have snow on their planet and that Antarctica seemed like a beautiful place to make a life. Slowly they came, ship by ship, landing in Antarctica. We watched for hours as the cameras from the ships around the continent filmed every craft. They landed and immediately started putting up habitats. Each one was a massive igloo, several stories tall, with several smaller living quarters surrounding it, all attached by walkways. At first no one could visit. We were told to give them space, and time to get used to life on Earth, so we did.

For the first few years it was wonderful. Scientists exchanged technology with the Rihn and our lives vastly improved. Some diseases were eradicated, sickle cell and cystic fibrosis never killed another human being. Our crops flourished in areas where they hadn't before, which meant world hunger was going to be erased as well. Earth was slowly turning into a utopia.

We also helped them to create a strong polymer suit to protect them from sharp objects when they travelled outside of Antarctica. They had fun with the suit, and eventually made them in different colors and started wearing them all the time. Antarctica had never seen so much color, and although we missed seeing their silver skin, it was quite cheerful. We were on our way to having nothing but electric cars when the Rihn's home world let us know they weren't happy with the asylum we had given their people.

I was seventeen when the attacks started. We were used to having their ships in orbit so when they came we figured more wanted to live on Earth. We didn't question it. But when it was clear the ships weren't heading toward the Rihn settlement, we got nervous. Things had been so good for so long, we forgot how bad it could get. The new ships were from the leader of their home world, and they crashed. On purpose, in very populated areas. The Rihn inside died instantly and soon blocks and blocks were covered in the same gray mist that Till had turned into. It was chaos and we spent the next week glued to the television, watching the carnage and praying for survivors.

By the time the first attack was over, and the mist cleared, hundreds of thousands were dead all around the world. California, Egypt, Africa, New Zealand, it was so random but that was the point. At last count twenty ships crashed into populated areas on the Earth. Jesk'ck was quick to tell us that during the attack he had received a message from the leader of their home world, Lord Tredaar. He learned about the exodus from his spies, and what happened to Till from a message Jesk'ck had sent the newcomers. Jesk'ck's warning had turned into a weapon for the home world. Tredaar was angry that Earth had given these "political terrorists" asylum and wanted to punish us. We didn't blame our Rihn. We knew they had nothing to do with these onslaughts and they were extremely helpful to every city that fell under attack.

They quickly invented a breathing apparatus that, when worn in our noses, would protect our lungs from the mist. It filtered the toxins in the Rhin's death mist so if we happened to breathe it in we wouldn't dry up and die. Unfortunately, we couldn't escape the slight purple tinge the mist gave us, but it was better than dying. It took quite a while to get the breathing apparatuses distributed around the world, free of charge of course. Thousands more died while waiting for them.

We got lucky, in my town we only had one ship crash and minimal deaths compared to most of the cities. Seeing some of my friends with purple skin was sobering. You never expect it to happen to you, to your town. And then it does, and everything changes.

The Rihn home world would send kamikaze attacks every few months. This lasted until we finally got the guns for the planetary defense system working. That took five years of round-the-clock work to complete. Five years of attacks from an enemy we couldn't defend ourselves against. I skipped college, wasting the scholarship I had won my sophomore year, and went to work in the factory. I helped keep the parts for the guns in order, then graduated to a welding position. My grandmother told her it reminded her of when her mother started working during World War Two. People coming together against a common enemy.

The work and attacks took a toll on humanity. Some began wondering, if we kicked our Rihn off Earth, would their planet stop attacking us? But whenever talk of kicking them off Earth started circulating on the internet, our Rihn would come up with something else to help us and prove their immeasurable worth. They found a cure to the purple skin and helped us mine for the metal we needed for the new planetary defenses. With them the production of the guns was completed forty percent faster.

The guns never missed a target, and the ships finally stopped crashing on Earth. But it wasn't perfect. Debris from the ships would rain down on the planet. We went from trying to survive the mist to hiding underground and reinforcing buildings to avoid the metal rain. Another five years and the planet-wide shield went online. If anything passed through the clear, shimmering shield without the United Nations' permission, it would be disintegrated. The planetary guns were now a backup and were barely fired after that. The next five years were spent watching ships crash into the shield. It made a shimmery pink and green light as whatever passed through it disintegrated. It turned into a favorite date night activity for the younger generation. The ones who didn't know an Earth without our Rihn. The ones who would never even think to kick them off our planet.

Fifteen years after the first attack, the home world finally stopped sending ships. It cost us millions of lives to keep the Rihn on our planet.

Years to finally perfect our defenses. I tell stories to my children what it was like before they came, and how much better it is now. They can't imagine a world that didn't have flying cars or healthy, affordable food. They ask about the long war, and I tell them how I saw purple humans and worked twelve-hour days on the guns. I tell them what the sky once looked like without the shimmering shield and I'm amazed at how they'll never see a pure, blue sky. But grateful for the light green they did see, because it meant we were safe.

But the older of us never stopped wondering, if the Rihn had never shown up, would we truly have need of such defenses? If we made the Rihn leave, would we be left alone? Would their home world find other aliens to align with and attack us? Aliens that could possibly get through our shield? It was the biggest question of the new age. No matter how much we loved our Rihn, it would be debated for decades to come. But all we can do is prepare for the worst and hope for the best. For Humans, and the newly declared Ourrihn, are allies against any foe that dare disturb our wonderful planet. Together, I know we will survive.

Rabbit Dreams

Jennifer Porter

When I was nine years old my mother moved us into Mike's single-wide mobile home. The trailer park's back side was a wooded wetland and peeper frogs symphonized the night after the ice melted in April. Mike had fixed the transmission on the beater of a car Granny had given us when my mother decided to hightail it out of Houghton and take on the life of a troll. That's what the Yoopers, those in Michigan's UP, call those that live below the Mackinac Bridge.

I was hoping to find my biological father. Granny was hoping my mother would finally make something of herself.

Sunday was the only day Mike could sleep in. Mom and I weren't used to guys that worked all the time. One time, I had to go to work with Mike because Mom had one of her migraines. When I got bored, Mike had me sweep with the floor broom, pushing grease balls, greasy rags, and greasy broken bolts into a pile. I did a good job, and the owner, Ralph, gave me enough coins for a Pepsi out of the vending machine. At lunchtime, Mike took me to McDonald's and let me play in the play place. I kept waiting for him to get crabby and yell about all the fuckin' noise but he never did. Still. Mom always said that anything too good to be true was simply waiting to fire arrows of disappointment into our hearts. I thought maybe Mike had those arrows hidden deep down inside his back pockets, the smoke escaping in thin wisps that trailed behind him.

And there was Mike, stumbling down the narrow hallway. "Trinity! The next time Wrangler wakes me up will be the last time."

I stuck my tongue out and rolled my large dark eyes, which he said were my greatest asset. He said someday there'd be men who got lost in my large dark eyes. Men in general grossed me out, but having them muck their way around inside my eyeballs gave me the heebie-jeebies, as Granny would say.

"Do not give me that shit if you know what's good for you," he said.

I didn't know Mike well enough to know if he were serious. Some of Mom's boyfriends had threatened to beat the shit out of me. There were also the pervy guys that iced over my neck hairs. My size-four mother, with skin so soft you're almost afraid to touch it but then can't stop touching it, was a hysterical whirling dervish, using any convenient household object (mop, lamp, coffee mug) as a weapon while she backed out of wherever with only her purse, her child, her dog, sometimes her suitcase, almost always in the middle of the night.

I stood there and watched Mike stomp into the master bedroom, bracing myself for husky shouting, then raced outside in my jamas and down the rickety stairs of the deck that leaned away from the trailer, hopping off the second-to-last step and onto a patch of dirt and crabgrass. Mike was going to fix the deck soon, now that we lived with him.

"Wrangler!" I whisper-shouted. "Be quiet." The black-and-white dog with pointy ears had his head down beneath a spruce, his paws scratching at the ground. He dropped onto his chest, his tail pointing at the sky. He barked until I was able to wrap my hand around his snout. He wrestled his face away, and I had to slap him on the rump before he quit barking.

I never understood why my mother's boyfriends always blamed me for her stupid dog. Once, we ended up at a shelter in Pontiac. And they don't take dogs at homeless shelters. Unless you are blind or deaf or have a doctor's note that the dog decreases your anxiety. Mom didn't have a note and I forgot to act deaf. My mother was smoking out the side of her mouth, staring at me and Wrangler as if she oughta just up and leave me for the pervy foster parents. We sat there in Granny's beater, in the parking lot, behind the shelter.

"Who'd take your dumb dog? Huh? No—body," she said.

"Stop blaming me for your dog! If you got out of bed once in a while maybe he'd know better," I shot back.

"That's not fair, Trinity, and you know it. I never asked to have migraines."

"You could go to a doctor," I said.

She looked at me like I was being ridiculous.

"Besides, it wasn't me who brought the pain-in-the-butt home from the Target parking lot," I said.

"But, he was sitting there all alone in a cardboard box, freezing to death. You saw him. Nothing but skin and bones. Everybody walked right by him. Like he wasn't whimpering. Like he was invisible." Tears welled up in my mother's eyes. "It was Christmas."

"He had a leaky eye."

She sniffled. "Yeah. An infected eye."

"Cost Granny a fortune in veterinary care."

My Mom hated being a major disappointment to Granny. I was sorry I'd said any of it. Whenever I hurt my mother it hurt like the days I woke up hungry and sat through school all morning without breakfast. I'd rather go hungry than hurt my mother.

Granny never reminded Mom of the money she owed her. She always said, "It's an investment in your future, Bambi, and Trinity's too. Don't worry about it." But my mother kept a tally.

Finally, Mom said to me that she was going to pay Granny back some day. I nodded. "He's the best dog ever, don't you think?" she said. Confidence was not my mother's strong suit.

I lied that he was the best dog ever. This made Mom ask if I loved her and that made me cry. Of course I did.

Mike's trailer had a little fenced yard and a tree for Wrangler to rest under when the sun was hot enough to melt candy bars on the sidewalk. Wrangler wrestled free and did a front-paw hop onto the same spot beneath the pine, scratching away, then he got ahold of something. He ran from me, whipped his head around, flung it, then came back and grabbed something else. I couldn't catch him before he raced off again.

"Wrangler, stop! Put that down. Come back here," I said, dropping to my knees at the spot beneath the tree. It was a clump of dried grass set in a small hole. I moved what remained of the top layer and found an empty nest. Not far from the nest lay two baby bunnies—their eyes still closed, their bodies dark slick gray, their tiny ears flat against their heads. They had pale pink noses with short white whiskers and the tops of their heads were practically bare of fur. When I poked them, they didn't move. Not even a little.

I stood up and ran to Wrangler. I grabbed his collar and dragged him up the porch steps. Inside, I pulled him through the dinky kitchen and down the other hallway to my teensy bedroom.

I shoved the dog onto the dog bed that Mike had bought when he'd decorated my bedroom. He had asked if I liked purple or pink or maybe turquoise and which Disney princess was my favorite and it took me forever to finally say— yellow, and the princess that loved books. I'd never thought about it before.

I scolded Wrangler. He lay down, his ears erect and his eyes sorry. I sat down next to him, the bottoms of my jamas muddy now, and wished I could call my father.

Rabbit Dreams

My father existed in my mind as fragments of what he might be like based upon what I was like and on the few times my mother ever spoke about him. It was similar to what happened when I came upon an unfamiliar word. I recognized the fragments that made up the word as those used in other words, and I could sound out the fragments—knew they were the building blocks of something new to understand. I'd write the word in a small notebook and at the library, I would find out its meaning and copy that into my notebook.

I always rode my bike to the library and Mike had attached a plastic milk crate with bungee cords to my bike for all the books I checked out. Sometimes, he looked through them too, especially the ones on animals and trees and the earth. He'd show me what he thought was cool. "Trin, did you see this?" Mom never understood the hiding-away-in-my-bedroom side of me. But I needed to spend time in places where it was quiet and in which my mind could go elsewhere.

I used to wonder if the quiet part of me was a part of my biological father also and I wondered about all those parts of him that were a mystery I ached to solve.

And then I remembered the baby bunnies.

After putting shorts on, I told Wrangler to stay and keep his trap shut and went outside. Already the sun wanted to stickify the world— the sides of the white aluminum trailer were sweating. I tiptoed to where Wrangler had been whipping his head around and searched the crabgrass. When I found a bunny, I crouched down, my butt resting on the backs of my summer-blackened heels.

Some of the rabbit's guts had poured out from a hole in its papery skin. It squirmed around, trying to get back to its nest. I stroked its head with the tip of my finger. I scooped it up and looked for the other one. The other one only had a little bit of blood on its haunch. After I picked it up, I saw the tear in its stomach. I could see its internals—pink and white and crinkly and shiny. The internals spilled out onto my hand.

I can feel the pain animals feel.

One of my mother's boyfriends had put a wild rabbit out of its misery after he'd hit it— saying, "Oh shit"—with his truck. He'd picked it up out of the gravel on the side of the road and with his other hand yanked on its head, breaking its neck. I cried out, grasping at my neck. The rabbit went limp and the boyfriend tossed it gently into the ditch. He wiped his hands on his jeans as he walked back to the truck, his eyes filled with sadness. We rode the rest of the way home in silence.

I took the rabbits back to their nest and along the way saw two more. Not together but not far from each other. I put the two hurt ones on top of the mound of dried grass and went back for the others. There was a fire spreading in my guts that made it hard to walk, made me stumble. I picked up the other bunnies one at a time and checked for guts or blood. One was still alive but had four puncture wounds that hardly bled. The dead one's head lolled back and forth while I cradled it. I took them back to the nest and gently set them and the other dead ones next to their brother and sister. As I was covering them with pulled-out grass my neighbor Alejandro lifted the chain-link gate latch.

"What are you doing here, Al?" I called him "Al" even though he didn't like it. I could never remember to say the "j" in his name as an "h" and it embarrassed me. When I said the "j" as a "j" in school the Spanish teacher rolled his eyes and corrected me until everyone laughed.

Al sucked his thumb, cocoa pebbles stuck to the front of his t-shirt, his pants refusing to cover his round belly. I asked Al what he was doing over at my house every time he came over. Well, Mike's house, really, I'd tell him. "Don't get too attached, we won't be here long,"

I'd say. He'd think of something we should play. Like pirates. Or my favorite: Charlotte's Web. I was the spider and Al the pig. This involved books, never Al's favorite game, but I'll admit, I tended to be bossy.

I was teaching him to read better, I'd tell his mother when she came home and found us sitting on the couch. We'd demonstrate and Al's mother would invite me over for dinner. Mom watched Al while his parents worked. I love Mexican food. Real Mexican food, like Al's mother made.

"Whatchya got under the tree?" Al asked. He had short thick lashes that reminded me of the floor broom at Ralph's Affordable Auto Repair, where Mike worked.

Al dropped to his knees. "What are those? Baby animals?" Yellow and green bits were stuck on his teeth and in the corners of his mouth.

"You're disgusting."

"Leave me alone. They taste good." He wiped his mouth with the back of his arm.

"Dandelions mixed with glue do not taste good." He'd convinced me to try it one time and the memory of the bittersweet chemical taste made me gag a bit.

Al leaned over and stuck his face close to the bunnies. "Ooooh, they're so little."

"Yeah, the stupid mother built her nest in a dog yard. Can you believe it?"

"What's wrong with them?"

"Some are dead. Those ones got bit. See." I pointed at the guts. "Fatally injured." I had to take deep breaths while my innards coiled and uncoiled, fighting each other for fresh air.

"What's fatally injured mean? What's the matter with you?"

"Never mind about me. They're gonna die. Their guts are hanging out. How are the guts gonna get back inside?"

"But they're still alive," he said.

"I know!"

Al and I stared at the three squirming bunnies.

"I bet it hurts," said Al.

"Oh yeah, it does!" I had to hold onto my stomach for several more moments, Al giving me the squint-eye. "They gotta be put out of their misery."

"What's that? You mean like exterminated?" Al's father sprayed bugs so he was always talking about "extermination" like it was a good thing.

"No, like put down. Like when a dog gets hit by a car."

"How ya gonna do that?"

I didn't know how I was going to do that. The bunnies' agony was passing right into me and searing my bones. It seemed like I carried a bag of tow chains around my neck, feeling the pain that was in the world. I scrunched up my shoulders against the sensation that someone was drawing circles with a sharp-pointed stick on my bare skin.

I wanted to crawl into bed with my mother and hide forever. If Mom were well she might caress behind my ears, tucking in my hairs while we snuggled together. It always made me feel sleepy and warm. But that damn Mike was in there.

"We could throw them in the pond," said Alejandro.

I narrowed my eyes. "Death by drowning is one of the worst ways to die."

We sat together on the grass. The air felt thick. My skin was nearly as brown as Al's and we liked to compare this by resting our forearms skin to skin. "It's my Indian blood," I had explained. "My mom says my daddy is part Ojibwa. She met him at the casino. My father doesn't know about me."

Wrangler barked, his paws up against the scratched, dirty windowpane, looking at me and Al. It seemed that his barking was like an earthquake shaking the trailer. I ran to the window and yelled, "Get down, bad dog!" He disappeared, but I could see the white tip of his wagging tail.

"Mike's gonna be mad if he gets woked up again," Al said. "That's what he said last Sunday when I was here. And the Sunday 'fore that."

"You think for once in your life you could tell me something I don't already know?"

Wrangler hopped up in the window.

"Goddang dog," I said.

"How come he won't quit it?"

"He wants the bunnies," I said. "Hold on." I ran inside and dragged the dog away from the window.

"Trinity?" Mike said.

I popped my head out of my bedroom. "Yeah?"

"Something going on I should know about?" Mike rubbed his stomach, his beltless jeans sliding down his meatless hips as he walked into the bathroom.

I had to push Wrangler back with my foot, bend down and shush him with my finger. I stepped out of the room, quickly closing the door.

"Somebody here?" he yelled from the bathroom.

I walked into the living room and stood with my side pressed against the small square kitchen table, shaking the jam jar of dandelions. "Just Al."

"How come Wrangler keeps barking then?"

"I don't know. Maybe 'cause he's a dog!"

He came back out into the hallway—the gray plastic walls lined with long strips of plastic. "You know, kid, I only get one morning to sleep in."

"I can't help it if the stupid dog barks!"

"I'm not so sure I buy that. Mostly I think you like it when he wakes me up."

I was stunned. Mike was always pointing things out I'd never thought about before. Like how the only person I hurt by not forgiving my mother was myself.

Or when he'd taught me how to ride a bike after he took me to the thrift store and we picked one out. He said the only one stopping him from being like a father to me was me. I'd fallen during the learning of the bike and had scrapes and I'd gotten angry and said things to him that shamed me still: words with pointy jagged letters that swirled red hot. Words that weren't ever true: I didn't need a father. My mother and I could make it on our own. He was a jackass like all the rest of them.

Maybe I did like it when he woke up. It was true that Mike made really good pancakes. He made some for Al, too. He watched Sponge Bob with us and laughed at the right times. He let Mom sleep in. He said she worked hard taking care of me and him and the house and Al, too. I rolled my eyes. Mike acted like being a family was a good thing. Like it was some kind of wish he wanted to come true. He was a soft piece of white bread with a hard crust. I felt sorry for him; he was going to get hurt worse than me. I knew already not to get too attached.

Mike looked at me then ran his hand through his hair, pushing his long curls back. "You gotta do something about it, Trinity. Or I will. That dog could get us into a lot of trouble."

I nodded while he went back into his bedroom, and after the door closed I could hear Mom ask if everything was okay. I wasn't sure what he answered. I wasn't sure what he'd do about Wrangler.

I ran outside and stood on the funhouse deck. The silver streamers Mike put on my bicycle handlebars were swishing in the wind and throwing rainbow glimmers against the side of Mike's shed. I looked at Al and thought about how his Mom and Dad said if they went to Cedar Point this summer, I could go with them. How Mom hadn't had a really bad migraine in a while. She'd been talking about taking college classes. Maybe she could get a certificate in court reporting.

Wrangler wasn't going to quit barking and couldn't go back in the yard with the bunnies there.

An idea came to me like a knock on the door. Mike had built a wooden box, set it on the ground on the other side of the trailer and filled it with dirt. Tomatoes, basil, strawberries, zucchini, and green onions grew in the box. Sometimes I helped Mike weed the box and the dirt was black like the insides of the black walnut seeds I smashed open with a hammer.

"Come on," I said to Al and ran to Mike's garden.

I waited for Al with a hand trowel in my hand. Nobody would ever dig down deep around the strawberries and find the little rabbit bones, and the decaying matter would feed the plants. It'd be like an offering. I bent over and dug a hole the size of my foot. "There, all set."

"What's that for?" Al said.

"Bury them."

"Like for a funeral?"

"Kinda." On my way back to the rabbits, a choking feeling began working its way up but I told myself that the pressure of the earth on their tiny bodies might feel comforting. They'd be together, too. I scolded the suffering of life and commanded it to stay behind me.

I knelt down and stretched the bottom of my t-shirt, creating a sling. With my other hand, I picked up the dead ones, one at a time, and set them inside the pouch. I had to take a rest, closing my eyes and listening to the wind rustle through the spruce needles. I scooped up each injured bunny and placed it on the top of the pile in my shirt. I made sure not to lose any as I got back on my feet.

I tried to keep my eyes on Al waiting at the box, but I began imagining the bunnies beneath the dirt—they wouldn't understand why this had to happen. They'd fight to stay alive. That's what living things do. Try to stay living.

"How come you're crying?" asked Al.

I shook my head and knelt down by the hole. I stroked each bunny with the tip of my finger, from its whiskered nose along the high ridge of its head then along its flat ear. I wished there was another way. I stayed in that space, stroking them, trying to puzzle my way out of this. Even if I managed to push their guts back inside, I didn't know how to sew up the holes. The guts would spill out as soon as they moved around. Al petted them too.

Wrangler wasn't a bad dog, really. He was just a dog. Dogs chased rabbits. He even barked at the birds to stay away, as if a sparrow could hurt anyone.

I laid each bunny carefully inside the hole. The breathing ones stopped squirming. They thought they were back in their nest, probably thought their momma would come back soon. But they weren't safe. I was going to hurt them worse. Great, big teardrops splashed down upon the slick gray rabbit fur. I grabbed the hand trowel and started throwing dirt inside the hole.

Al knelt down. "Gosh, burying them alive." He used the side of his hand and helped hurry the soil into the hole. Al and I packed the dirt down by pressing the flats of our hands on the mound.

Then Al whispered to the mound, "Sorry. We had to do it." He sat up and looked at me. "It'll be over soon."

He patted me on the head as if I were a stray dog. It made me feel better despite that it annoyed me. I was glad Alejandro was my friend.

I hid the burial mound with the strawberry plant suckers. I felt the black soil snake its way down the rabbits' throats and into their lungs, stealing their breath. The earth pressed down on their ribs, cracking their fragile bones and crushing their organs. The top of my scalp throbbed with a pounding intensity. I cried out, stood, and ran, then collapsed in the yard.

It was very quiet down in the blades of grass. My heart thumped and I smelled earthworms, sunshine, and dew. I imagined the earthworms tunneling far below, replenishing the soil with their castings—as Mike had explained. Life giving back to life.

A car went by. Another child yelled hello to Alejandro. When I turned over, my eyelids showed blood-red to the sun. The ground slightly tremored with Alejandro's approach. He asked if I was dead. The wind lifted my bangs then set them back down. Sometimes I thought it would be better to be dead. To not feel anything at all. Just be inside the blackness and quiet. My friend bent down and placed his small, soft, brown hand on my heart. The screen door to our trailer banged open and heavy feet pounded down the deck stairs.

Mike shouted for my mother then Mom shouted from the deck.

I kept my eyes closed. I thought about the baby bunnies realizing I had played a bad trick on them. I wanted to bury my bag of tow chains in Mike's yard. The first time I ever saw Mike's trailer, the porch light and the lamp that sat on the table in the center of the trailer's wide end window were on, shining out into the winter night. "He's waiting for us," Mom had said.

Mike swept the hair off my face while I rested in the grass, and the way he said my name, as if I meant something to him, something he could not stand to lose, made me open my eyes.

DOC BISHOP'S BROKEN HORSES

ANNA O'BRIEN

Llewellyn brought his own shovel to dig the grave, partly because he couldn't bear the thought of nine-year-old Belle Samson digging it herself and partly because he knew Mr. Samson didn't have a decent tool to his name. Mostly, however, Llewellyn brought a shovel because he felt it was his own fault that the Samsons' had a dead horse on their hands.

As Llewellyn dug deeper into the dark earth he could hear Belle sniffling behind him. He would have preferred the girl not be around to witness every second of this somber ritual, just as he would have preferred the damned dead horse's eyes to remain shut instead of staring wide open at him while he dug. Stubbornness was a trait of both the living and the dead.

"Doc, you think Chief's in heaven now?" Belle asked, idly plaiting the dead horse's creamy mane, seemingly oblivious to the bullet hole between its eyes. Llewellyn was thankful of the early spring season—no flies yet.

"Oh, I'm sure of that," he answered. He paused digging to wipe his brow. "Belle, would you mind hollerin' after your ma for a glass of water? I've worked up quite a thirst."

Llewellyn watched as Belle solemnly marched to the back of the Samsons' small slatted house, her red braids swinging with determination. Then he looked over at Chief, flat out on his side. Bloat hadn't set in yet but the body was stiff with all four legs jutting out like he'd simply been tipped over.

A pretty palomino, Llewellyn had said why sure, that looks like a fine horse for Belle when Mrs. Samson had him over a week ago. Mrs. Samson said she found the horse for sale one county over and it seemed like a deal—a child-proof seven-year-old gelding for how much? Too good to pass up, darn tootin', Belle proudly announced when they brought the horse home and had Llewellyn look at him.

Of course Llewellyn was in no official capacity to evaluate the horse. People in Rockwood had collectively come upon the habit of calling him Doc for no other reason that he could fathom other than he was quiet-natured and gentle with his hands and that seemed to suit most animals. Llewellyn bashfully declined to respond to this honorific until one day when Mrs. Connors screamed out her front door, "Doc!" when her beloved Jersey was having trouble calving and Llewellyn had come running without a moment's hesitation. After pulling an enormous breach bull calf with half the town watching and smiling to themselves, Llewellyn finally allowed himself to answer reliably to the title.

Rockwood didn't have a veterinarian anyway and the last time old Dr. Hemp, the physician, got near a horse with the intention of doctoring it, it kicked him in the ribs, which he had to wrap himself because no one really cared much for him and offered no help.

Mrs. Samson came out to the grave with her daughter and a pitcher of water. Belle went right back to the corpse's mane, braiding and securing little blue ribbons that matched the ones in her own ginger hair.

Mrs. Samson, in her stained and worn blue-and-white-checked apron, made a wide berth around the horse and bent over the hole to hand Llewellyn the water.

"Belle says you think he had a twist," she said, wiping her damp hands on her apron.

Llewellyn nodded. "I reckon so. Just seems odd, a young horse like this."

"You're the one who shot him?"

"Yes ma'am."

"Well," Mrs. Samson paused, looking off to the horizon where the sun was setting. "When my potatoes come in, I'll be sure to put away some extra for you."

"I'd appreciate that."

Mrs. Samson turned to walk back to the house. Llewellyn pulled out his pocketknife, climbed out of the hole, and bent over Chief. He neatly cut one of the braids off and handed it to the girl.

"You think of him up in heaven now. Put this somewhere safe. Now go on back to the house with your mother. It'll be dark soon."

Belle took the braid and paused, looking at Chief and then at Llewellyn. "I did love 'im, you know," she said, then turned toward the house. "Doc Bishop said he could tell how much I loved 'im when we bought 'im."

Llewellyn resumed digging and although it was getting dark he was in no hurry. Why should he be? There was no young, beautiful Alice at home anymore to greet him, only his small herd of Herefords and his own horse, a nag named Sas, an animal that should've been shot years ago only Llewellyn didn't have the heart.

He looked over at Chief in the last of the sun's rays. The rigor had pulled the horse's dry lips back into a terrible grin and the large, yellow, slanted incisors caught Llewellyn's eye. These were not the teeth of a seven-year-old horse.

Llewellyn stepped across the hole for a closer look. The teeth appeared filed or burned, making the horse appear younger. Why hadn't he looked in the horse's mouth when the Samsons bought him? Why was he content to just look from a distance? His fault it was, then. A horse trader swindled the Samsons. And this is what happened.

He'd tell Mrs. Samson in the morning. Then he went back to digging, the shovel shouting against the rocky soil as he worked alone in the dark.

***

Walking to the saloon the next evening, Llewellyn could just make out the freshly dug grave in the Samsons' back yard and a familiar sensation returned to him. He could feel his feet start to drag and sweat bead his brow from the effort of lifting his legs. He was becoming heavy again.

A common sensation before he met Alice, this heaviness would come and go and would sometimes be so acute he was unable to lift himself from bed. When Crum Sr.'s steer bled to death after Llewellyn couldn't stop the hemorrhage from a broken horn, his left leg dragged the ground for a week. When he shot Harbaugh's rabid dog, he couldn't raise his arms to the point where he didn't eat for two days.

In fact, when he met Alice, Llewellyn was in the midst of a heavy fit, as he had taken to calling them. It was the night Cal Offutt's colt became wrapped in the very barbed wire fence Llewellyn had advised he take down a month earlier. Every move the young horse made wrapped him tighter in the rusty wire, biting into his flesh and making him scream a scream that was heard clear across town so by the time Llewellyn arrived, twenty people had gathered to watch.

In the futile efforts to untangle the poor creature, Llewellyn's hands were sliced to ribbons. After he shot the horse, he found he couldn't raise his hands to wash them. That was when Alice stepped out of the crowd, took his hands, and said, "What a mess of a thing. You did what you could," and bandaged him up.

When Alice took Llewellyn's hands in hers that first night, he felt his heaviness dissolve. He could lift his shoulders and march his legs. Five months later, they were married and for two whole years Llewellyn not once felt the weight of Rockwood upon him.

This evening, Llewellyn could hear the piano tinkling before he entered the saloon. He smiled, thinking it was a bit early for Josie to be playing, but when he pushed through the double doors, he was surprised to find a stranger at the upright.

Cash Smith saw Llewellyn enter and motioned for him at the bar. Josie stood behind the bar with her square jaw set and her hands on her wide hips. Ina was busy swarming the rowdy group gathered by the piano, most of them strangers.

"Mr. Deputy here says he ain't gonna do nothin' 'bout those new boys over there," Josie said to Llewellyn as he pulled up a stool. She poured him a drink.

The younger of the two men, Cash Smith, rolled his eyes over the rim of his glass, already three-quarters empty. "Llewellyn, I done told her two things. One, they ain't doin' nothing wrong. And two, I cain't do nothin' even if they was."

Josie huffed. "Ain't doin' nothin'? I'd say they was over there banging on my piano, causing a scene. Plus—" She squinted over at the group. "I just don't like the look of 'em."

Llewellyn looked over at the group. The middle-aged man playing the piano wore brightly polished silver spurs and a large tan cowboy hat with one raven's feather held captive at the brim. With a large black mustache that concealed most of his mouth, he sang off-key, his hands in competition with his voice for what body part could produce the most cacophony.

A handful of other men, all dusty with pinched eyes and rough skin as if they'd been baked in an oven, gathered around the piano swilling drinks as fast as Ina could get glasses in their hands. Occasionally, one of the men would swipe at Ina as she turned away. She giggled and flashed her large, toothy smile until she saw Josie, Cash Smith, and Llewellyn watching her. Ina's eyes fell on Llewellyn and her face flushed. She looked away.

"You gonna let her act like that?" Cash Smith asked Josie.

"She's old enough to take care of herself," Josie replied, though Llewellyn could tell she was upset.

Llewellyn remembered when Josie, surrogate mother to almost every young, foolish person who wandered into Rockwood, took pale, frail, but hard Ina under her care years ago. The woman—a young girl then—had come off the train looking for relatives that had never been in Rockwood to begin with. With no home, no family, and barely enough English to communicate, the German immigrant squatted in an abandoned silo for three days until Josie dragged her out and put her to work at the saloon.

"Who are they?" Llewellyn nodded at the piano.

"Oh, he don't even know that!" Josie rolled her eyes and glared at Cash Smith. "What kind of sheriff's deputy are you?"

Cash Smith went red and pretended to search for something in the bottom of his empty glass, his bushy dark beard holding a few crumbs from dinner.

Llewellyn was about to defend his neighbor and friend when he felt a hand on his shoulder. The music had stopped.

"Is this the Doc Llewellyn I've heard so much about?" a deep voice boomed behind him. The air around Llewellyn suddenly reeked of whiskey and the smoke of a recent campfire. Turning around, he found himself staring at the coal-black bottlebrush hanging above the upper lip of the piano player.

"Just Llewellyn's fine," he replied. "And you might be?"

"Well, I might be ol' St. Peter, or I might be Methuselah," the man said, setting his shoulders back. His menagerie of stringy friends laughed. "Or I just might be the Virgin Mary!" He winked at Josie who snorted in disgust. Howls of laughter threatened to blow the slats from the walls. The piano player let the laughter die out, then said, "I'm Doc Bishop. At your service." He held out a large callused hand and gripped Llewellyn's too tightly and shook it for too long, all the while staring hard into Llewellyn's brown eyes.

Llewellyn rescued his crushed hand. It fell to his lap. "Where you all from, Doc Bishop?"

A half-sneer twitched the corner of the other man's mouth. "Oh, here and there," he replied. "On the road quite a bit." He looked expectant and Llewellyn kindly obliged, asking the obvious question out of politeness.

"You a traveling physician, then?"

Bishop smiled, showing an expanse of tall teeth similar to the white keys of the upright. "'If you have men who will exclude any of God's creatures from the shelter of compassion and pity, you will have men who will deal likewise with their fellow men.' St. Francis of Assisi, patron saint of animals. I'm fixin' to be the first veterinarian this area has seen."

Ina came up to the bar. "This town here's already got a horse doc, Doc Llewellyn." Her pale blue eyes darted between the two men.

Bishop considered Ina's bosom. "Now, honey, that's what I came to see the man for. I just wanted to see his credentials."

"Credentials?" Josie spat. "Ain't no one around here needs any credentials except for the law and the railroad. We trust Doc Llewellyn with our lives and have no use for two horse docs."

Bishop pulled a yellowed folded paper from a worn leather wallet. "Ever been to France, honey?" he asked Ina. She squealed. "First ever veterinary university's over there. Trained scientists." He looked at Llewellyn. "Parlay voo Francay?" He replaced the yellowed certificate before Llewellyn could get a look at it.

Llewellyn, whose education went to the fourth grade, had a mouthful of words but couldn't move his tongue to push them out.

"Course we sell horses, too," Bishop continued. "Got some real pretty ones we've been saving just for Rockwood folk because ain't nobody have but nice things to say about y'all. In fact, don't you fellas think this young lady would look just riveting on that black colt we got out there?"

Bishop's posse gave a collective affirmation. Ina's eyes widened. "A horse for me?" she asked.

"I thought you was afraid of those things," Josie said.

Bishop grabbed Ina's chin and lifted her face to his. "Your white hair against his midnight coat would be like moon glow—simply magical." Ina blushed.

"Anyway," Bishop said, turning back to Llewellyn. "Nice to meet you all. We'll be coming through officially tomorrow. Straight down Main. Won't be able to miss us." He gave Ina one more glance, then stood and, with the rest of his cohorts, exited the saloon.

The room filled with silence as soon as the double doors swung shut.

***

At noon the next day, a dust cloud formed toward the east. The Rockwood townsfolk heard a rumbling like thunder and some said they felt the ground shake. Little Belle Samson was the first witness as she hosted a tea party for her Raggedy Ann dolls and she abandoned her guests to run down the narrow dirt track from her house to watch the wave of horses and riders enter the town.

Bishop and his group galloped down Main Street as promised. Dispersed among the riders were perhaps a dozen other horses. Through the dust you could see a few paints, a leopard Appaloosa, bays and chestnuts, a roan, a draft horse, and an onyx black colt. A chorus of hoots and hollers joined the cacophony of rumbling hooves so that by the time the group reached the saloon in the center of town almost all of Rockwood stood along the street.

Llewellyn stood in the pharmacy restocking his iodine and soaking salts when Bishop's horse slid to a halt just outside the door. Llewellyn watched out the window.

"Ladies and gentlemen of Rockwood," Bishop called in a deep, loud bravado. "Do your horses have hives? Do your swine have sores? Are your lambs lame?" He spun the chestnut he was riding in a tight, fast circle. With the leather reins in his right hand, he extended his left arm out wide. The other horses fidgeted nervously. "I, Joseph Bishop, doctor of the science of veterinary medicine, am here in Rockwood to offer my unique services to those in need. Was it not Proverbs that said a righteous man regards the life of his beast? Look to me as a messenger. With medical advances straight from Europe, I shall heal thy wounds." He lowered his left arm and stroked the chestnut's wet neck.

Through the pharmacy window, Llewellyn could partially see the crowd that had gathered. Many wore skeptical faces. Josie in particular had a scowl pulling down her mouth as she crossed her large arms in front of her apron.

"Why, this spotted colt here we rescued from a tribe down south." Bishop pointed to the leopard Appaloosa. "Just skin and bones, he was. But after a few days of my special tonic and liniment rubs he was sound as a bell and strong as an ox." One of the other riders goaded the Appaloosa to trot in a tight circle. Llewellyn watched the animal move. Although it was difficult to make out details with the fast movement of spotted legs, he thought the colt looked off in the hind. Just as quickly as he noticed, the man yanked the colt to a stop.

"We also offer fine horses for sale," Bishop continued. "Only the best across the area: saddle broke, sound, and ready for whatever your needs may be." Another man trotted out the black colt whose eyes were so wide with anxiety the whites were like boiled eggs. The flashy colt pranced and flagged his thick dark tail.

Another rider paraded the draft horse, an enormous bay with high white stockings and thick feathering down each leg. "This here draft would make you a reliable work horse on Monday, show horse on Saturday, and church horse on Sunday," announced Bishop.

"How much for the draft?" someone yelled.

Bishop smiled and white teeth peeked from behind the curtain of his mustache. "All inquiries can be discussed at my camp, just outside town." He looked through the crowd. "It will be my pleasure to serve you."

Then, with a holler that startled humans and horses alike, Bishop slammed his spurs into the chestnut's flanks and the group took off at a gallop down Main Street, leaving the crowd shielding their noses from the dust.

Llewellyn pushed his way out of the pharmacy, the bottles of iodine like bars of lead in his arms. He brushed past Belle standing on the corner, her small hands curled into fists.

"Doc!" she yelled as he passed. "That's him! That's the man that sold ma my dead horse!"

Llewellyn turned to look back at the girl, whose face was ablaze with injustice. "I know it," he said as another invisible weight was added to his arms. He hunched over to bear it and continued walking.

Anna O'Brien

***

"You ever deal with horse traders?" Llewellyn asked Cash Smith the next night as the two men bent over draughts at the saloon.

Cash Smith shook his head. "Can't say I have."

The clink of dishes filled the lull in the conversation. Llewellyn watched a lonely wisp of smoke from a patron's pipe slowly uncurl in front of them. Llewellyn was sleeping a lot but not well. His calves, just weaned, were lowing through the night for their mothers, a deep sound so saturated in despair Llewellyn took his rifle the previous night, stood on his porch, and fired three shots at the moon to spook the young momentarily out of their misery.

Dragging his feet back to bed, he thought of Alice and how she hated spring weaning and how, sometimes, he would wake in the middle of the night alone in bed and walk out to the fence where he would find his wife kneeling, talking to the calves that gathered near her, soft ears pitched toward her gentle voice. She would sing them lullabies meant for their first baby who was lost in the womb and created a grief between the couple that would have turned into a black, palpable entity had they not had each other to tease apart the weight and share.

Josie appeared behind the bar. "We cain't have that kind of folk in this town. No one needs any more damn horses and we already got a vet. Ain't that right, George?" she yelled to the booths in the back. A grimy older man in faded overalls tried to hide behind his mug.

Josie looked at Llewellyn. "George here was telling me the other day he had a litter o' piglets out of his best sow that had pneumonia. He was fixin' to call you over to take a look. George?" she called over the din. "George, how them piglets doing now?"

"Oh just fine, Jo," George's companion called back. "That ol' Doc Bishop fixed 'em right up! Gave somethin' to that sow, too!"

Llewellyn watched as George fumbled to throw change on the table and leave.

Josie's eyes blazed. "George!" she yelled as the man hustled out of the saloon. "Damnit, I swear!" George's companion laughed himself into a coughing fit back at the booth.

"Well," Josie said, flustered. She vigorously wiped the bar with a rag then looked at Cash Smith. "You know where they stayin'?"

Cash Smith shook his head.

"Someone said they've set up camp down at ol' Crum's place. Big campsite, bonfire, horses all over. Now, I know ol' Crum Sr.'s been dead and gone for years but that don't mean just anyone can set down on his land. That's private property. Them's squatters."

Cash Smith sat there looking at Josie, his big eyes blinking slowly.

"Well, you in charge till the sheriff come back, ain't you?" she asked.

Cash Smith's complexion turned from red to purple, a chameleon of mortification. "Well, I just figured . . . ." he sputtered.

Josie's cynical eyes softened. "Sheriff stumbled outta this here saloon three weeks ago and hasn't been seen since. A town's gotta have law and order, Cash Smith. Folks need an authority figure. If they realize there ain't one, well . . . ." She filled Cash Smith's glass. "I'm just thinkin' we need you to do somethin' about these squatters, that's all. Nothin' fancy."

***

The decrepit animal stood tied to a post, a front leg bent to rest a swollen fetlock. Llewellyn watched the horse doze, its lower lip drooping so that it almost touched the ground.

"Hope you didn't pay too much for her," Llewellyn said to Steiner, who bought the nag two days prior.

Steiner grumbled, uncrossed his arms, and spat his chew. "Doc, I swear this thing was fit as a fiddle. That ol' Bishop swore this mare weren't more than four, sound as a bell, and full of piss and vinegar."

"Mind your language!" Mrs. Steiner barked as she walked up to Llewellyn. She handed him a steaming loaf of bread and a bag of cut greens and radishes. "Here you go, Doc." She nodded over to the horse. "So, what you reckon's wrong with it?"

Llewellyn ran his hands over the roan coat. He felt the mountains and craters of a skeletal landscape barely covered by hide. He felt a hot, swollen fetlock and a thready pulse. Listless, the horse allowed Llewellyn to pry open her mouth and have her pink dry tongue pulled to one side.

Something about the horse's teeth reminded Llewellyn of the palomino he buried days ago— charred, uneven edges, not the teeth of a four-year-old.

"You know, George's piglets died," Mrs. Steiner told the back of Llewellyn's head. "Every last one of them. Sow, too."

"Hush, woman," Steiner snapped. "Doc ain't here for gossip."

"Oh, you hush yerself," Mrs. Steiner replied, shooing her husband away with her hands.

"Doc oughta know. If he'd a treated them pigs, every one of them would still be here." She gave Llewellyn's back a knowing look. "That Bishop. I don't know about him. Somethin' about him and his group." She wrung her apron with her hands.

Llewellyn's arms, which were already shaking under their own exaggerated weight plus the weight of the horse's head, collapsed. Llewellyn struggled to fill his leadened lungs with air. The horse's head, so quickly released, fell in a sickening arch, teeth clattering at the knees.

Llewellyn backed against a fence post for support. The couple looked at him. "All right, Doc?" Steiner asked.

Mrs. Steiner glared at her husband. "Course he ain't right. He ain't been right since—" and she caught herself and looked at the ground. "Well, he's tired. Folks like you wear him out, ain't that right, Doc? I'll fetch you a glass of lemonade and an extra jar of jam to take home. Goes well on the bread."

As Mrs. Steiner turned toward the house, Steiner put a hand on Llewellyn's shoulder. "So, Doc. What you think's wrong with this here horse? Can you fix her?"

Llewellyn shook his head. How do you fix age? How do you put back together something that's already been bastardized? Llewellyn slowly worked up his heavy answer when a woman's scream electrified the air.

Both men looked toward Main Street, two blocks over. "What in the hell?" said Steiner when a second scream followed. The older man took off running in the direction of the commotion, leaving Llewellyn trying to gather himself and his strength, just to stand, just to lift his head, just to breathe. One leg at a time, one joint at a time, he moved as if in a bog.

By the time Llewellyn made it to Main, there was no need for explanation—everything played out step-wise, as if rehearsed. Llewellyn saw Ina on top of Bishop's black colt. He watched her blonde hair, undone from its usual braid, let loose as a yellow flag behind her as she uncontrollably galloped past. At once her body listed to the side as the half-wild colt took a sharp turn. Then she slid almost gracefully onto the dirt road as the horse bucked and bolted and continued to gallop away as if the world was ending and he was attempting to be the first witness.

The screams stopped. Several people ran to Ina's still body in the road, her petticoats crumpled and one leg bent at an unnatural angle.

"Llewellyn!" Steiner yelled. "Come quick!"

Llewellyn dragged and pulled and heaved his body toward the group. He knelt by Ina's head, her face pale as the moon and just as cold but when he touched her cheek, her pale eyes fluttered open.

"Stay quiet now," Llewellyn said and moved his hands to her leg. The small crowd gasped in unison.

"Is it broke, Doc?"

"Can you fix it?"

"How bad she hurt?"

Questions quivered above him as he found two breaks—one below the knee and one in the hip. "Where's that damn physician?" he asked to no one in particular.

"I don't want that quack touching my Ina," said Josie, bosom heaving from running. "You set it, Doc. Like you did that one ram. Healed real nice."

After the group created a stretcher out of an old feed bag and carried Ina to the back of the saloon, Cash Smith arrived.

"Bishop's saying his black colt is gone. What happened?"

"That bastard put my girl on top of that creature knowing full well what'd happen!" Josie yelled. "She don't know a thing about horses and he put her on a wild one and now he's crying that his horse is gone?" Her voice crescendoed and she threw her dishrag on the floor. "Damnit, Cash Smith, ain't been nothing but mischief since that group rode in here. Now I ask you again, what are you going to do about it?"

Cash Smith paled at Josie's fury, her round face red and sputtering, salt-and-pepper hair springing out of her bun at the nape of her neck.

Someone handed Llewellyn a board torn from the back porch to use as a splint. As he straightened the leg with a pop, Ina's eyes flew open and she sat up.

"Mein Gott!" she cried and grabbed at Llewellyn's hands.

"Easy now," he said and pushed her back. He thought of her as an injured swan with her pale white legs and long thin arms.

Human. He hadn't worked on a human since Alice. He swore he'd never touch another human again. He wasn't a physician. He wasn't trained. One book. That's what they had. Alice found it in her classroom, a childbirth book for midwives, illustrating proper positioning of the baby and what to do if it were breech or the mother too weak to push.

They had joked, Llewellyn and Alice, during her second pregnancy. They had to joke after the first miscarriage, had to cautiously celebrate when she made it to the second trimester. Alice said, "Think of me as one of those old cows out there," and she tossed her pretty auburn head out the bedroom window to Llewellyn's pasture, to the mountains and beyond. "Soon I'll be big enough you can just feed me from the trough." And though her ruby mouth smiled and danced with laughter, in her gray eyes Llewellyn saw fear.

Labor came quickly, rushing through Alice like the train on which she arrived in Rockwood. Llewellyn was at her side with Josie, who was ordering a sulky Ina about to fetch towels and water. When the birth wasn't progressing, Josie looked at Llewellyn. "You sure you don't want to step outside?" Llewellyn shook his head, afraid for his wife and terrified for himself that if he let go of her delicate hand, if he stopped fiddling with the wedding band that sat loosely on her thin finger, all the weight in the world would come crashing down on him, in him, and he'd fall to the ground, unable to rise.

Josie called the physician in from the saloon. With a disinterested peek, he concluded Alice needed more time to dilate. They should wait. Then he left, looking at his pocket watch.

Time crawled and Llewellyn watched his wife grow weaker. He thumbed nervously through their book, wincing at drawings of where to cut and how to stitch up a woman.

At the physician's second visit, the man placed a yellowed hand on Llewellyn's shoulder telling him to wait out the night and he'd re-check in the morning. Llewellyn knew that if you wait until morning with a cow, when the sun comes up you've lost both mother and calf.

Llewellyn asked Josie for the sharpest knife she had. He asked Ina for iodine, all the towels she could find, and for catgut suture in his supply drawer. Llewellyn roused Alice from her stupor, so weak and pale she looked like parchment, and told her, "Easy now," and she smiled, but those gray eyes betrayed her.

The book didn't tell Llewellyn what to do with so much blood. It didn't elaborate on how to piece together diseased tissue. The instructions on how to revive a blue baby were cursory at best. When the physician arrived the next morning, the room was empty. He found Llewellyn sitting on the porch, his back propped against the wall. Llewellyn looked at the physician, unable to lift his arm. "Can you help me, Doc?" Llewellyn pleaded. "I can't stand up."

The physician looked down at Llewellyn. "Who the hell do you think you are?" he asked, and then walked out, leaving Llewellyn panting for air as the weight pushed down on him.

***

Llewellyn couldn't get out of bed for three days after he set Ina's leg. Townsfolk worried. People brought food. Breads and pies stacked up on the kitchen table, more potatoes and beets than he could ever eat piled up on the front porch. Someone cut a handful of newly sprouted crocus and arranged them in his bedroom. Josie came twice daily to clean up and force him to eat.

"I think Ina's turned the corner," Josie reported the afternoon of the third day. "I told her she ain't ever gonna walk like she used to, but she's able to sit up now. She said she's gonna make you twenty pounds of stollen when she can. Says you saved her life."

Llewellyn laid on the bed in a cold sweat, his eyes static to the distant purple mountains outside the window.

"Cash Smith paid a visit to Bishop," Josie continued. "Managed to write up an eviction notice." She shook her head. "I'm guessin' that didn't go over too well since he came ridin' back at dark, the notice crumpled in his hand. I swear, that boy."

Calves lowed in the sunset. Josie busied herself with dusting and Llewellyn heard her chop potatoes in the kitchen. After a while, she returned.

"Some people been sayin' they want you as the new sheriff." Her eyes searched Llewellyn's body for a reaction. The thin mattress sagged under his weight and the frame buckled. Josie noticed the odd trail Llewellyn left behind as he shuffled away from Ina the other day, more snake than man as he dragged both feet, leaving deep ruts. The shoes by the bed were scuffed and trampled.

"Me, I'm not so sure you can handle it." The sun sank behind the mountains, leaving an orange glow. A cold breeze stirred and rattled the single-pane window. "But someone's gotta get Bishop to take his leave."

When Josie left and the breeze stopped knocking and the calves went quiet, Llewellyn fought the bed. He pushed and pulled and sat up with the effort of Atlas, arms shaking. Each progressive movement, however, became easier as his resolve solidified. Boots on, stand up, move forward, close the front door.

The crescent moon dangled like an ornament in the night sky by the time Llewellyn dragged himself to the fringe of Bishop's camp. A large orange bonfire crackled in the center and Llewellyn could see the light jump off silhouettes of rugged men. He heard the soft sounds of horses settling in for the night.

Just before Llewellyn stepped into the camp, he hesitated, realizing it was well past midnight. He had no gun, no horse, no plan. He heard voices and instinctively dropped to the ground in a heavy heap. There he lay, partially hidden by the soft, sweet-smelling timothy grass, and listened.

". . . think we got a few more sales round these parts . . ."

". . . I catch you selling another colt for that cheap, I'll whip your ass . . ."

"Hell no, I don't speak German . . ."

"You don't need to speak it to get what you want . . ."

Llewellyn closed his ears to the rough talk and gazed up at the indigo night. He felt ashamed, lying there, hiding, unable to move. Even the animals in the sky he felt he betrayed; Ursa minor searching for its mother, Canis major run off. And Alice up there somewhere, watching.

Suddenly, Llewellyn heard the men rise.

"All right, I think it's hot enough," he heard Bishop say. "Go get me that old yellow mare."

Llewellyn pressed himself into the earth as a man walked near to fetch a horse. Returning to the bonfire, the man said, "I ain't holding this one like we did the others. Almost had my god-damn fingers tore off."

"You sound just like a woman," Bishop snapped. "Grab hold of that ear and don't you let go."

Through the tall grass Llewellyn watched as Bishop pulled a hot iron poker out of the fire. Bishop walked toward the horse, pulled her tongue out and to the side, and pressed the glowing metal to the mare's front teeth.

There was a hiss and for a moment everything was quiet until the creature smelled the smoke from her own burning flesh. She gave a scream that penetrated Llewellyn's soul so deeply he was barely able to clamp a hand over his mouth in time to stifle a wail before it climbed out of his throat and over his lips.

"Hold her now, damnit!" Bishop yelled and continued to hold the hot iron to the teeth. The horse shook her head and tried to strike with her front hooves. Someone hobbled her by tying a rope to her left front ankle and she almost fell. Finally, Bishop removed the iron and stepped back.

"Come on, now, darlin'," he said. "I just took ten years off yer life. Yessir, that's a fifteen-year-old mouth now, not twenty-five. Go on and take her back now. Give her some water."

The same man as before led the horse back to the others who were now agitated. Llewellyn rolled to his side and the man looked over in the direction Llewellyn lay, no more than twenty feet away. Llewellyn froze. The man stood listening intently, his right hand hovering over the gun on his hip. The grass in front of Llewellyn's face swayed with each panicked exhale.

After an eternity, the man turned and walked back to the bonfire. He did not leave the mare any water.

The men at the camp went back to their conversations and drink and Llewellyn's heart slowed from a gallop. He turned in the grass so he lay on his back. Again, he stared up at the sky. He found Pegasus cantering north toward the mountains, looking lame on the hind. His tears came slowly at first then raged down his face. He cried for Bishop's mare and her burned teeth, he cried for George's sow and piglets, he cried for Belle Samson's dead palomino, then for Ina, then for Alice. He left a few tears for himself at the end, an economy of self-pity. When he was finished, he found the night quiet and the camp asleep. The bonfire had shrunk to the gossiping crackle of embers and the horses were still.

With Herculean effort, Llewellyn stood. With the same plod as before, he dragged his broken soul back home, leaving a rut in the dirt road behind him.

***

Back in bed, Llewellyn couldn't sleep. He stared up at the dark ceiling and listened to the occasional calf low and as dawn broke he listened to the birds. When he heard his old nag Sas rustle in the paddock, he decided it was time to move and lift the weight for himself.

It took a long time to dress. His lead legs had to be picked up and placed into his pants by arms equally heavy. Llewellyn abandoned breakfast. Dragging himself to the paddock, he was able to saddle Sas but found he was too heavy to pull himself up into the saddle.

He yelled for Cash Smith.

Rushing over still in his bedclothes, his neighbor looked worried. "What's wrong, Llewellyn?"

"Help me up on this here horse."

"Is there an emergency somewhere?"

"In a manner of speaking, yes. Now go on and help me up."

Cash Smith tried to give Llewellyn a leg up but found Llewellyn to be of stone, too heavy to heave.

Cash Smith stood back, slightly embarrassed. "Hang on, now. We'll need more help." He looked at the sky. "I know it's early, but I'll go round up some folks. You stay right here." He patted Llewellyn on the leg reassuringly, a fatherly motion, something Llewellyn had never seen Cash Smith do. "We'll get you on your way."

Soon, Cash Smith returned with half the town's menfolk. Murmurs of "hey Doc" and "how you doin', Doc" rustled the still morning air. Cash Smith took the lead, directing someone to hold Sas at the head, someone on the off side of the horse to hold the saddle, and a few people on the near side to hoist Llewellyn up into the saddle as if he were a sack of bricks for the railroad.

Every person there, on the count of three, felt the weight of Llewellyn, although each felt it differently. Cash Smith felt it in his heart, Bill Haughs felt it in his gut, and Crum Jr. felt it in his hands. Not one of them there could believe it took half the town to get one man on a horse.

Sas grunted with the weight as Llewellyn settled into the saddle. Cash Smith tightened the girth. "All right now, off you go."

Llewellyn looked at each of the familiar faces below him and he saw Josie making her way up the drive. He nodded appreciation to the group and pointed Sas west, urging the old horse into a canter. Sas faltered for the first few strides, adjusting to the weight on her back, then obediently picked up, creating a wake of dust.

Josie arrived when Llewellyn was a spec in the distance. "Where's he goin'?" she demanded, her hair not yet pulled back into its requisite bun.

"Emergency," said Cash Smith. "Prolly a calving or something. We helped him up."

Josie shook her head. "Ain't no one out in that direction, Cash Smith. You know that."

Self-righteousness fell from the deputy's face. "Bishop's camp is out that way."

Josie nodded.

"What you think he's fixin' to do? Think I should go after him?"

"I don't know, but if you don't go after him, I'm fixin' to find a horse and go after him myself," Josie growled.

Cash Smith balked as his resolve faltered. He turned to the small crowd. "Imma need a horse to borrow," he said to no one in particular. "And—" He looked after the galloping dot in the distance. "Anyone who wants to come with me, I'd appreciate it."

Minutes later, Cash Smith and four others sat atop a ragtag herd, all misfits purchased recently from Bishop. Crum's red mare was lame on the forehand and Harbaugh's gray gelding had an oozing sore on his haunches.

Josie looked on proudly at this assembly. "That's right," she nodded. "Do what's right by this town and by Doc. Our Doc."

Cash Smith pulled the reins on the paint he sat astride and led the group down the road. Some wives gathered behind Josie, still tying their aprons on and putting their hair up for the day.

"God looks out for the meek, the lame, and the sick," someone murmured.

"No, Llewellyn does that," Josie snapped, and walked back to the saloon.

'TIS I, I AM HERE

Sarah Yasin

There are some women whose men come home to them every day. This is not a story for those women.

***

Sumner rowed his dinghy into the dark green waters of the cove while there was enough daylight left to add a leathery tone to his sunburned arms. Hair shielded his neck from the sun, and only the slit between his beard and baseball cap shadow had turned red.

He checked the plastic bag at his feet to be sure the pebbles were still dry. He had to make his offering before the Lady came out for the night. He didn't mind bringing her offerings, as long as he didn't have to look at her face. She wasn't ugly or anything, she was actually quite elegant, but he hated the sight of scorned women.

***

He first encountered the Lady when he was fourteen. He had taken the dinghy for a ride around the island and lost track of time, unaware the sun had set until he saw the beam from the lighthouse across the cove bidding fare-thee-well to residual hues fading from the vast horizon. The moon would soon shine enough to light the way, but he promised his mother he'd never go into the ocean at night.

He pulled the boat ashore and flipped it over, not worried that anyone would take it since everyone in Newagen knew it was his. It was the most decrepit boat on the island.

He clambered to the dirt road at the edge of the beach and heard a soft clanging over the steady breath of the tide. He sensed someone was looking at him while the clangs grew louder, as if getting nearer to him. He turned around and screamed in a voice-changing shriek when he saw a woman with iridescent skin wearing a long pearl necklace reach her sleeveless arm out to touch him. At the same moment he screeched, she recoiled in disappointment.

Clearly she thought he was someone else.

"Uh, lady, uh, who ya lookin' for?"

The woman, slender and dressed in a tasseled gown, grimaced and turned back to the beach and strolled into the water. As the jangling faded from the baubles on her dress, he watched her glide deeper and deeper, thinking she must be unhinged going for a night-swim in her clothes. When she submerged her head and made no sign of swimming, Sumner ran after her. "Lady, 'taint so bad! You don't need to end it all!"

She emerged on a sand bar in front of a giant rock in the middle of the cove. He stopped dead and watched her scale the rock like she was ascending a staircase, somber and melancholic. He stood at the edge of the shore gazing at her as she paced across the ledge, turning her face away from him every time she scanned the beach. He watched her miserable wandering until he felt sick to his stomach and ran home, stopping at the dirt driveway to catch his breath. Fighting down the image of the despondent lady on the rock, he grabbed a clam hod from the front yard. He went into the woods and gathered pine cones and arranged them in the wooden hod.

He slipped into the house and put the basket on the kitchen counter. His mother called from upstairs, "That you, Sumner?"

"'Tis I, I am here, Ma."

"Where's the dinghy, dear?"

"Left it at Hendrick's Head."

His mother came down the stairs in a velour housecoat and curlers in her hair. She put a kettle on the stove. "Like some tea, dear?"

"Ayuh, nice idea, Ma." Sumner took out a package of melba toast from the cupboard and laid it on the table. "I got you some pine cones, wanted to give you flowers but it was dark." He gestured to the clam hod.

She walked to the arrangement and ran her fingers along the handle. She put a hand on her son's face and sat down. "What kept you so long, dear? See the ghost of Hendrick's Head?"

Sumner's eyes widened and the kettle squealed. He brought her the teapot. They sat at the table, and that night Sumner learned the legend of the lady of Hendrick's Headlight.

***

Dipping a fragment of melba toast into her tea, Ma said, "Your great-grandmother was among the witnesses one evening in 1929 who sighted a strange woman at various points on the island. Dressed to the nines, she was seen walkin' along the center road, then later along the beach that leads to Hendrick's Headlight. Everyone said she seemed out of place since one does not wear a mink stole to the beach." She winked at the boy and continued. "Some of the locals offered help, asked her if she was lookin' for someone, and she just walked past them in a daze. Next mornin' her body washed ashore in the cove beside the lighthouse. Some old hens involved with the Village Improvement Society collected donations to give her a burial with a simple headstone reading 'UNKNOWN LADY who washed ashore at HENDRICK'S HEAD.'"

Sumner bristled. "I bet they wouldn't'a given her a burial were she dressed in rags."

Ma leaned back and smiled at her child's insight. "On certain nights when the stars are especially bright, the figure of a slender woman dressed like an old-time socialite can be seen walkin' along the brink at Hendrick's Head. Fishermen have seen her, but they can't get a very good look cos when she comes out, it appears all electrical finery stops workin'. Boat lights fail, radars go haywire, even the new streetlights on the road to the beach flicker and turn off."

Sumner put down his cup. "Do you think the Lady was a woman scorned like Aunt Mildred?" Stories about Aunt Mildred haunted Sumner partly because of her sorrowful fate, and partly because of his fear that insanity could be hereditary. Aunt Mildred lost her mind after spending years at the railing of the neighbor's widow's watch, waiting for her sweetheart to return back from a night of fishing. Her self-care declined as her obsession with waiting turned to severe mental anguish. She died from anxiety, but Sumner thought she should have smoked some pot to calm her writhing nerves. Sumner's mother insisted pot couldn't help someone like that because pot is a depressant. "What if she smoked before she had a chance to get sad? Like every morning?"

His mother's answer: "Seems like a lot of work to not feel sad."

Sumner spent long hours sitting pensive in the blueberry bushes in the back lawn for a week following the encounter with the Lady. He took a ride around the island, and had no idea the words he would utter to his mother that night when he came home would set off tiny cells of cancer growing in her stomach. He slid his shoes off in the garage and bellowed the usual greeting as he entered the house, "'Tis I, I am here!"

He found his mother in the drawing room, looking at the television and cradling a pile of tobacco in a rolling paper over her lap. He pulled a hundred-year-old ottoman in front of her and sat on it. "Ma, whoever the Lady wants isn't worthy of her. 'Tain't right letting a nice lady wait and wait like that. I'm goin' to start bringing her things, things like the little tokens you sometimes want, to take her mind off him."

His mother stared at the wall and her chin gave a quick tremble. She stood and tightened the belt on her robe. She reached down and caressed her son's face, then stepped outside to smoke the cigarette she'd been rolling.

***

Around his nineteenth birthday, Sumner's mother said she felt abdominal pain the morning his brother failed to come home after a night of fishing. He argued mightily with Hiley the previous evening before he launched the boat they recently inherited from a kindly neighbor. The last words he heard from his brother were, "Ma didn't lose Father to the sea—he ran off! Lost at sea my arse! He was tired of bein' tied down in Newagen. She doesn't want us to go boatin' at night because she's paranoid we'll head down to Portland and make a decent livin' away from her. She thinks we'll leave her, too."

***

Her pain increased, leaving her curled in bed, unable to get through basic daily tasks. They couldn't afford a visit to the hospital, so Sumner made a clearing in the woods and grew pot plants to help ease his mother's pain. He'd roll the buds into joints and take them upstairs to her on a tray as if they were aspirins. Sometimes he toked with her, but mostly he watched her writhe as she sat up to smile at him. This went on until the day he found her collapsed in a heap on the floor beside the bed. She was dead. There was no money for a cemetery plot, so he scraped together what he could to keep her ashes in an urn on the mantel.

He picked flowers to put by the urn every few days, but something odd started happening in the house. Weird sounds. Window shutters flapping open and shut. Growls from the cellar.

***

Sumner was never particularly adept at hygiene, and when the noises began, he got worse. He stopped shaving and maintaining his haircuts. He bathed only in the summer months when he went swimming, and took what the family referred to as a whore's bath standing in front of the sink in the winter. He wasn't so much averse to taking care of himself as he was totally and completely terrified of the twitching spiders that collected in the tub. He swore they were speaking to him.

Held in a locked gaze at the multitude of twitching insects, he sensed they were imploring him to take action. Mesmerized, he believed they were telling him to take care of the Lady: if he performed small gestures for her they would go away, but only when he did a Grand Gesture would they stop bothering him permanently.

Until he could figure out a Grand Gesture, he developed a habit of performing small gestures—piling pebbles in neat stacks like cairns around the headlight, planting lupins across the beach for her. One night the noises in the house were particularly bad. The growls from the cellar rose up in scales, changing from the nightmarish howl of a bull moose to the terrorized yelps of chickens being taken by a fisher cat.

He knew the spiders were causing the clamor and it would only get worse if he didn't take action, so he got out of bed and went into the dark woods out back to gather pine cones into a plastic grocery bag. He tied the bag to seal it, and then laid it in the dinghy and rowed to the beach where he saw the Lady. She was strolling along the ledge where the silhouette of the lighthouse stood against the night sky. He placed the pine cones in a row on the rock in the middle of the cove, and the Lady walked off the ledge and fell into the icy water. Like a ghost ship that leaves no trail in its wake, her plunge made no ripples or splash in the ocean. He hoped she was coming to see his offering, so he bent down to straighten out the cones and felt cold drops on his back. He looked up to see if it was raining. The Lady stood over him, water falling in beads off the wrought tassels of her dress. He was afraid she might try to seduce him, but she only stood there, staring.

Being sufficiently wigged out, he rolled away from her and slinked into the dinghy. He was safely back at the landing behind his house when he realized he hadn't been using oars the entire trip back—instead he used his thoughts to steer the boat like Hiawatha sitting upright in his canoe.

***

In all his thirty years, Sumner didn't have a reliable income. He survived doing odd jobs and peddling fish to local tourist traps. Most mornings he went around to the various restaurants on the mainland and tried selling them the fish he caught, but only rarely would they indulge him out of pity. The folks who did offer help were quiet about it, and not one member of the Village Improvement Society was among those who helped.

The taxes on his ancestral home were low, and the township held a hearing every spring over whether to waive the taxes for him. They always decided in his favor until the spiders started talking to him. He appeared in the town hall all smelly and crusty for the hearing, and a wave of nausea swept the hall. While the residents of Newagen were generally charitable, his newfound funk made them less inclined to pay for his share. For the first time they decided he had to pay—and it wasn't a large sum. They agreed to lower the assessed value because of the presence of an outhouse on the property, even though he had a proper bathroom inside the house. This put the bill at $200 for the year, an amount that would take him years to come up with. Some of the more gracious residents worried it would drive him away; force him off the island and onto the mainland where people wouldn't be so caring to him. Only a few dared voice their fears and protested in downeast accents. Sumner stood to make his case and was struck still by a forceful whisper in his ear telling him exactly how to make a Grand Gesture for the Lady.

The town council stared at Sumner's frozen stance as he listened. If he could do exactly as instructed, the tax bill would go away. Someone noted a seagull had perched in the rafters. The bird shouted, and while Sumner heard instructions, the people heard the gull's incoherent calls.

Someone in the crowd stood and said, "That gull wants to pick at the trash in Sumner's beard—let's close this motion so we can shoo them both out."

***

The following day Sumner went through the house clearing things out in the event the town seized his assets. There wasn't much apart from a television, a coffee maker, and his mother's costume jewelry. He opened her jewelry box and took out a diamond tennis bracelet, diamond meaning glass. He held it up to the dusty sunlight and looked around the room until he saw tiny prisms cast through the jewels. He knew his father had given the bracelet to his mother before he disappeared, but he didn't know why she never wore it. A seagull perched on the windowsill and wailed, "This belongs on the wrist of a lovely woman."

He wrapped the bracelet in a napkin and grabbed a beer from the fridge. On his way out the door he caught sight of a cluster of spiders in the corner of the ceiling. They said to him in their non-verbal telepathy, "You and the Lady are meant for each other. Go to her. Godspeed."

He finished the beer in the dinghy on the way over, taking breaks from paddling to take sips, but one beer wasn't enough to dull the pain in his arm muscles. When he arrived at the rock it was low tide so he could pull the dinghy onto a sandbar and walk up the rock.

He took the bracelet out of the napkin and laid it across the top of the rock. He looked across the ocean to see the sun setting and whispered, "'Tis I, I am here." Then, obedient to his mother even after her death, he hurried to the dinghy to get home before night fell. Rain started falling as he pulled the boat onto the back lawn.

***

The next night the noises came back with violent fury. He heard banging in every room, as if furniture were being tossed around. Then he heard an ungodly clanging against the window and looked to see a glowing string of pearls knocking against it. It was the Lady, floating outside his bedroom. When he ran to the window to let her in, she looked at his face and turned in dejection. She fell to the ground, and crawled away in a sad slither. Sumner reckoned what an awful long walk it was to his home. The Lady was never seen outside of Hendrick's Cove—for her to travel all this way must have meant something special. Then it came to him: she was looking for him! He was the one she was waiting for, even if she didn't recognize him as such. As soon as this epiphany came to him, the racket in the house stopped. All was silent again.

***

Believing he had a legendary destiny, he breathed in deep a great sense of peace. Tomorrow he would do the Grand Gesture, the instructions he received at the Town Hall all made sense; he knew exactly what to do. But he needed to rest and build strength, so he smoked a bowl to go back to sleep.

***

The following morning he got up and took a bath, changing the water as grime dissolved off him. He put on a pair of socks and went through the house nude looking for the things he needed for the picnic he would share with the Lady that night. He checked the coffee can under the sink for extra cash, but it only had three dollars in it. All he had to do was sell some of his homegrown herb to tourists on the mainland, but he needed cash today, and couldn't wait for nightfall to peddle his weed.

He went outside to check on his crop of marijuana, still dressed only in socks, and a family of tourists on bicycles zoomed past. The mother growled something about not looking and calling the cops.

Into a clam hod he gathered candles, plates, cloth napkins, and two drinking glasses. He spent a long time in the bathroom trimming and shaving his massive beard, shaping it into a dapper Fu Manchu, and then removed all of it. He put on a suit—meaning black jeans and a tee shirt with the graphic of a tuxedo on it.

He rowed to Palumbo's Corner Store and gathered up the essentials for a romantic supper on the beach: Moxie and beef jerky. For dessert, peanut butter wafer snacks. The Lady was going to love it.

He took his items to the counter and asked the clerk to start a tab for him.

"Sumner, you know it's not allowed."

"Oh come on, Mary, you know I'm good for it."

"Actually I don't, Sumner, which is why it's not allowed."

"Mary, you're a nice girl, and I'm sorry but I really need this stuff tonight."

"I think you're nice, too. I like you without the beard, almost didn't recognize you." The clerk looked up as new customers filed in through the back door and Sumner clutched the items and ran out the front door.

"Sumner! Cripe, Sumner!" She ran to the doorjamb and yelled without running after him since there were customers in the store. "I hate to call the cops on you, but you leave me no choice! Sumner, bring it back! Ju-das Priest!"

Two of the customers ran after him, but Sumner jumped into the dinghy and rowed feverishly toward his home to put his pursuers off track. He saw the two head back into the store, and he swung into a cove and rested. He waited for what seemed to be the amount of time to gripe about the theft and make a purchase and leave. To disguise himself, he tied a

cloth napkin around his head. He draped net-
ting over the gunwale to disguise his boat, then
rowed back toward his destination. Once he
was out of view of the store, he slowed his pace.
He needed to store up energy for his date.

He arrived at Hendrick's Head and laid out
the picnic on top of the rock. He was most
pleased to see the bracelet was gone, taking it
as a sign of acceptance from the Lady. When
the sun set he lit the candles, but they burned
down to the bases while he waited. It was an
hour after the candles went out when he
cracked open the beer. He wasn't accustomed
to six-packs, just the occasional one or two,
and he had to urinate frequently. To save time
in case the Lady appeared, he took off his pants
and underwear and kept them in a pile close to
the place settings. That way he could keep an
eye out for her and pee off the rock without the
ceremony of undoing his tight jeans. It was a
balmy night and as the beer started to kick in
and warm him, he decided to take his shirt off
as well.

He passed out in the early morning hours,
too drunk to feel the sun scorching his totally
naked body. Intense light reflected off the water and burned through the layers of his skin.
Gradually children's playful shouts came from

the beach, though they were muffled from Sumner by a wall of inebriation.

Three children swam out to the rock and climbed it to find Sumner's beet-red, exposed body splayed on the outer edge, an indistinct crimson lump to the folks at the beach. They hollered and hurried to the beach to tell their parents about the scary naked man on the rock. The coast guard was called. Sumner was too hungover to move.

The coastie arrived, an overweight woman with ruddy skin. She tried to lift him to incarcerate him, but he was badly burnt. Her grasp on his shoulders smote him, the sting spread down to his feet. He opened his eyes in a squint, but sunlight blinded him while sublime pain shot across his skin. He screamed, destroyed by the mistaken idea that the assault on his shoulders was the Lady come to jilt him. With a defeated whimper, he flopped off the rock and into the icy needles of the ocean. He didn't reemerge.

The large woman panicked and switched on the radar to locate him. The small coastguard vessel puttered around the cove as she franticly checked her instruments. After a few minutes, she turned the motor off. With trembling hands, she logged a report of an unidentified man being sucked by the undertow to a benthic level of the ocean floor, far out to sea.

The children and their parents stood lined along the shoreline, waiting for the indecent man to reappear at the surface of the water, to be pulled up by the coast guard like an illicit lobster trap full of black, crawling, pinching creatures. The grownups watched as sentinels, their children mute with fear.

The coast guardian paddled to the somber shore and beheld abject expressions of torment, imploring her for respite. Casting aside her failure to rescue, she assuaged the distress of the stricken onlookers by announcing the undertow sucked him down to an unreachable low seabed, and there was nothing to worry about from the likes of him.

At this, the beachgoers should have sighed and resumed their picnics and swimming. But they remained standing, soundless, waiting for the man to reappear.

***

Some people feel constant peace in a pedestrian manner, not even knowing its presence. There are others who stand and wait, surrendering their souls to the ardor of a ghost.

VITAMIN FOR THE SOUL

Emad El-Din Aysha

And still, after all this time,
The sun never says to the earth,
"You owe Me".

Look what happens with
A love like that,
It lights the Whole Sky.

—Hafiz

"Look at that. What does it remind you of?"
Dr. Kanji Li had just put an orange effervescent tablet into a half-filled glass of water.

His esteemed colleague Dr. Yingluo Mika shrugged her shoulders. Her hair was like dark cords draped on the white expanse of her lab coat, as spotlessly clean as his own. The skirt she wore beneath the coat was black, just as were his trousers.

"The sun dissolving into the sky," he said triumphantly.

"Isn't that what we're going to do here, Kanji-san? Drown away the sand. Turn it from the red planet to the blue planet to, eventually, the green planet."

"Please, Kanji is enough. It will go from the planet of war to the planet of peace. A second Earth, with *your* magical touch." He groped for her fingers. She pulled away respectfully but stood her ground.

They glanced off the white metal scaffolding holding them up in the space station, down on to the dark side of the planet, with its little clots of light and humanity, scattered across the Martian landscape.

"Then we can finally settle down, set roots, and feel some real gravity for a change," he said.

"I'd be a grandmother by then."

"You *will* be a grandmother, just not up here," Kanji insisted.

"Yes, but who will be my suitor?"

He sighed in silence but smiled inwardly nonetheless.

***

"The skies belong to the Japanese, the lands to China. This is as fair a bargain as is possible," the gray-uniformed ministry official told his youthful assistant.

"But why not both for us, sir?" His assistant was dressed in green work clothes, reminiscent of a military uniform, with a slight grayish hue.

"Because we have enough troubles of our own down here," he said, looking out at the factory floor from his metal-plastic office. The Uighur workers were busily churning out respirator units for the exploration parties mapping the planet and testing the soil.

"In that case, would not our own laborers work better? We would not need an interpreter, at least."

"That is the whole reason why we are here, so we do not have to use interpreters back home."

"But respectfully, what has the Uighur to do with Mars?"

"What has the Uighur to do with Syria? The last Great War the world fought, that we fought, was with the likes of these, mobilized from camps round the four corners of the Earth. We can ill afford another. None of us."

"But we won the war, sir."

The ministerial official dragged his gaze away from the shop floor to look out the window of the factory dome, where they worked and slept, to the hostile terrain beyond. "Won by the skin of our teeth. We have become too accustomed to green hills and city gardens. We are in a desert, and no one tames a desert like a nomad." He turned to look at his assistant, as if to scold him. "And never underestimate their spirit or ingenuity. We can make compromises when need be. How else did we pry Mongolia from the Russian grip? And they are helping us with their horse-rearing and yak-herding skills here too. So we will share the glory of winning Mars. There is no shame in this. Better Japan with us than against us, and with the Americans."

His gaze rose to the stars, in search of a metallic star shining in the night sky above.

***

Kanji was attempting to order his jumbled thoughts. "Mars Terraforming Platform One," he said out loud to the computer that was obediently jotting down his words. "Atmospheric convertors are pumping oxygen into the air, changing the mix of gases to match Earth's composition, but the air is dissipated with the Martian storms. We need water, fresh water, in quantities unimaginable, to dissolve the salt in the sands and purify the soil to make it ready for agriculture to produce oxygen on a scale that the oxygen-to-carbon-dioxide mix will become sustainable."

He stopped momentarily. Everything depended on everything else in an indefatigable circle. Trees and forests were needed as wind traps to break the reign of the storms. But they in turn needed water. Everything depends on water. The planet was saturated with it but the water was saltier than those of the deepest oceans on Earth.

"Desalination would take forever," he found himself saying out loud. "Life on the planet's surface is impossible without the hydroponics here. We need greenhouse gases to start warming the planet's atmosphere with the power of the sun and generate rain that is not salt, alkaline, or acidic. But that, in turn, demands moisture on a planetary scale . . . ."

The sound of his office door opening distracted him. "You need to eat if you are to think clearly." Yingluo entered, bringing a sugary snack with her from the local mom-and-pop shop.

"Thank you," he said as heartily as he could. He scooped up the treat with a pair of biodegradable chopsticks. "You know, this would go nicely with some tea."

"Yes it would." She left it at that.

He munched away, having become used to these awkward silences. When he was sure she was finished he said, "You are the astrophysicist. I am the lonely botanist and ecologist."

"First in my class. My thesis was on how to detect gravity waves. I corrected Einstein's equations. And you were the first in your class too."

"Do not remind me. Nothing like this has been done before. Growing some spuds inside a shelter on Mars is one thing, changing an entire planet is another. We cannot roof the skies in plastic. There is no measure for comparison." He sighed, then said, "Where would you go shopping for water, fresh water, in the solar system?"

"Shopping! Because I am a woman?"

"I did not mean it that way. It is just a figure of speech," he explained apologetically. "But where *would* you get the water."

"Earth is out of the question. We do not have enough fresh water there as it is. And the sea levels are declining, everywhere. Two options. Well, three actually."

"The more options the better," he replied.

"First, produce the water locally, from hydrogen and oxygen, taken from anything, rocket fuel, from waste material, from the Martian soil itself if need be."

"A good idea but too expensive. The electricity needed to fuse oxygen and hydrogen into vapor is too laborious. Separating hydrogen from water for fuel is too expensive on anything but a laboratory scale for us to go and reunite it again to make water. That is why we are still wedded to petroleum after all these ages."

"I know. May I continue, please?"

"Of course." He gave her a sheepish grin.

He could imagine such a conversation in Communist China. Japanese women learned from their counterparts' habits over the Age of Rapprochement.

"Second, a risky and time-consuming option. Harvest the water from comets. The water on Earth itself is from shooting stars."

"Fascinating and picturesque. I could imagine our space station docking with an ice harvester on Halley's comet. But would it not be easier to redirect the comet to crash into Mars."

"You stole my thought Kanji-sa—Kanji. That is my third option, but with modifications."

"You are serious."

"We do not want to wait forever for a comet to approach the Martian orbit. We have the asteroid belt. At the same time we do not want to punch giant holes in the atmosphere or cause gigantic earthqu—Marsquakes or erupt dormant volcanoes."

"Then it is a question of finding a way to bring the water into the atmosphere, slowly, seeping into the Martian air," he asked expectantly.

"Precisely," Yingluo said. "A controlled burn or another method. The rains will do the rest of the work. And we can harvest water from the asteroid ice up here, store it, process it, funnel it down in measured quantities over time."

"We must coordinate with our colleagues below," he said with excitement.

"We must coordinate with *their* colleagues back on Earth. This is more than moving mountains. It will take a political will greater than it took to win the last war. And we must have all of the calculations ready from now on if we are even to convince our superiors, here, that it can be done. May I use your computer?"

"It is not 'mine' any more than this station is mine. I simply utilize it. I will go and get myself some tea. There is still the taste of saccharine in my mouth."

She did not make a comment or an expression. But he could see a smile forming behind the veil of her pitch-black eyes.

***

"But why horses and mules? Are not mechanical vehicles faster?"

They were working tirelessly on into the Martian night, their bodies still not in synch with the rotation of the planet. The ministry official was sitting behind his desk as his assistant typed away instructions into the computer. His master was obscured by the dark, with only the lower portion of his face illuminated in white by the solar-charged desk lamp.

"The animals are cheaper and easier to fuel and maintain. We have solar power but the panels are still made on Earth from expensive materials we have yet to find here. That is the mistake the American makes. And we harvest the meat and milk and manure and hides of these beasts. One day, one of these days, we will let them loose onto the Martian plateau, where they can graze and reproduce at will, chased by predators we will also bring with us, to keep their numbers in check. We will turn the land into savannah, governed by rainy and dry seasons. Then we will also set the savannahs on fire."

"But why would we do . . ." the assistant realized that he had spoken out of turn, and bowed in apology.

"A brush fire is *good* fortune. The saplings cannot reach the light because of the old brush above them, and the carbon replenishes the soil. Death is part of the cycle of life. Black following white into gray, into black and white again. You would think the young longed for this, to replace the old."

"Never, sir. We all stand on the shoulders of those before us." He bowed again.

"Do not fret. Our cocooned existence on Earth has made us overlook these facts. Ultimately it is the plants and animals that will inherit the Martian soil, bringing effortlessly with them the balance we so dearly seek and so seldom attain through our technological follies. Then and only then will humans follow, beginning with the nomad."

"The nomad first, sir?"

"Yes. Do you know how the Mongol beat his enemies in our distant past?"

"Respectfully, no sir."

"You are too young for your job," he almost snapped at his underling. "By traveling farther in the remotest deserts than anyone else dared to imagine. The Mongol drives two horses, both mares. One to ride to death, one to keep in store for when the first expires, with the rider living first off the milk and blood of the mare and then its flesh when it finally dies."

"That is terrible, sir," the younger said.

"It is 'efficient.' Nothing goes to waste while the objective is attained. But we are too humane, too soft and corpulent like our own horses to see this. The Apache did much the same. Fortunately for us the American has forgotten his frontier ways and the memory of his efficient enemies. We will use those we have to spread out, faster than anyone else, then we will settle down and turn the planet into an oasis in the night sky and for the horses of the very same nomad. Let us just hope our Japanese allies can figure out 'how' in due time."

"But what are we doing here on Mars to begin with, respectfully. Is it profit alone that we seek?"

"We are here to change the face of the future forever. The American reads only his own people's histories, when he reads history at all. He thinks war is inevitable. America is in decline, like Athens, and so Sparta 'must' wage war against it to ascend to the throne. We do not think this way, nor should we. Do you know the story of the great advisor who told a king not to fight the larger enemy plotting and preparing against him?"

"We took it at school, and again in the army. An outsider, a scholar, was given charge of the armies. He forbade them to engage during the first battle. The same with the second battle. The enemy, arrogant with his presumed victories, became negligent and attacked the smaller force for a third time, but by then the larger army had become exhausted, with their supply lines too stretched, and were defeated easily by the smaller force that had become courageous and confident, evading the enemy the past two times." He fell silent for a moment. "We are here to exhaust the American?"

"In a manner of speaking, if it comes to that. The American has no reason to come here. His land is too big, his life too luxurious. He has no reason to 'uproot.' He will only come here in force if he believes he has to, out of jealousy of his rival. And he will spend more money than he needs to convince his people to come. Our population is begging to come. To escape the beehives they live in, the influenzas that kill millions, leaving those alive permanently maimed, the synthetic foods they are forced to gobble down. They will pay *us* to come here. And what will they do? Who will come? The engineer in search of scrap metal to recycle into engines and bridges. The cultivator in search of clean soil to grow soy and tobacco side by side. The chemist in search of pure substances to process into usable objects. The porcelain maker in search of new ceramic combinations. The corn farmer, in search of land that is his own, not rented from another nation. The man who wants more than one and three quarters children. The woman who is afraid she will lose her husband or boyfriend to the more fertile, foreign neighbor. Women in search of a single husband. 'These' persons will build the future, turn the sands green, build our towns, and *civilize* the nomad, with time. By then the American will have spent all his father's savings and polluted his land beyond recognition. The homeland will prosper and will feed our people to become tall and strong like the American. Our industries will thrive and give us the navy and airpower and satellites we need to shelter ourselves behind a mobile Great Wall stretching from Earth to the skies. With Mars a giant base of operations in the heavens, there will be no room for error and peace will prevail. *Now* do you see why we 'have' to be here?"

"Will we ever see home again, sir?"

"Not in this lifetime. But our bones will be buried with our ancestors. You have made savings for this?"

He nodded, respectfully.

"Again, this is something the American cannot fathom to save for. Least of all the flower of his youth, drowning in a sea of student debt. *We* carry our abode wherever we go with us. The American is too uprooted in his own abode. That is why he cannot win, and he cannot even win over our allies to his side." His eyes shifted upwards once more, dragging his face out of the limelight of the desk lamp.

The assistant resumed his duties, checking production quotas, as his superior's machinations were enveloped in the dark.

***

"Your idea, it was not half bad," Yingluo said.

"Which idea was that?" Kanji said.

"Building a giant greenhouse round the planet. That could be done, you know?"

"But how? I was only joking." He went suddenly silent as the implications dawned on him. "I see! You mean like the rings of Saturn."

"Yes." She was overjoyed. "We can have rings of Mars, made of an ice belt. We will use them as wind-traps to capture the lost moisture of the planet that the gravity cannot keep below. Then use them to reflect light back down to heat the atmosphere. The larger asteroids we will crash-land, very carefully, onto the planet's surface, to create oceans. Oceans of fresh water to purify the sand, on your process which we will name after you." His eyebrows went up. His firewalls were not as good as he thought. "Then to be populated with plankton and seaweed and coral and fish and crabs and lobsters that will breathe life into the air. Other shooting stars we will burn in the atmosphere, very carefully, to avoid holes in the ozone layer we are seeding onto the planet's skies, which will introduce even more moisture. I have the calculations all ready, thanks to the cooperation of 'your' computer."

He patted the machine with pride, clad in white plastic with a dark screen and black metallic keys. "Your first name is Yingluo?"

"Yes, a Chinese name in origin. My mother gave it to me. She learned it while taking Chinese cooking lessons."

"It means jade, am I correct to assume?"

"Precisely. An allusion to a string of jades in a necklace, like truths following each other in an argument of pure reason. And Li is a reference to reason, and 'to set in order,' with roots in Chinese."

"You have been doing your homework," Kanji said, unsurprised.

He paused himself before adding, "Mikao is Japanese for new moon, is it not?"

"My father wanted me to be an astronomer, like him. He always felt his name had destined him to that fate. So my mother found a scientific name to her satisfaction. And your name is similar to the Greek *cosmos*."

"But it not as poetic as the Chinese," he replied. "And I have found myself working beneath the stars, like my own father. Do you know what my grandfather said every Japanese man's dream is?"

She pursed her lips, exposing two perfectly spaced dimples in the creamy white of her skin. She was weighing his response.

"To live in an American house, marry a Japanese woman, and eat Chinese food."

"Do you know what *my* dream is?"

He did not venture a guess.

"To marry a cosmonaut who lives on the ground!"

***

"Look, look!" The ministerial representative pointed to the black expanse of night sky, from his seated position in the wheelchair.

His assistant, now sporting gray temples, watched as the first balls of ice began to turn to fire. "Blue to red to blue. How can this be possible, sir?"

"Our allies have realized who is more useful to them in the future."

"The data they downloaded to us, it says they will also position balls of ice around the planet."

"Like pearls in a necklace, beautifying the neck of a desert bride."

"And warming the desert with moisture till it is a desert no more," his assistant continued, less poetically. He was now wearing an Uighur coat over his green-gray uniform. It kept him warm in the cold Martian night.

The ministerial representative coughed. His lungs had ingested too many homegrown cigarettes over the years. The stress of the job was finally getting to him. "First order of business, once the fireworks are over. We have guests to chaperone round the planet. The company employing them, the company responsible for the space stations, wants to build Japan-towns on the old Chinese model, in our underground cities!" He almost laughed out loud.

"It will never work. They will be absorbed by us, sir. Even the Uighur has come around to our ways."

"The Japanese knows how to divide his mind between what is domestic and what is foreign, but as long as it helps him be creative in our aid, who are we to complain? You must give others some space to thrive. A horse cannot grow to fruition in a cage." He read through the tourist manifest. "Oh my goodness."

"What is it, ministerial representative?"

"I wish to house this middle-aged couple in my *own* home. Imagine that from me, and I cannot abide the smell of rice wine. Still, they are to be honored guests wherever they go. Is that understood?" He said sternly, with a fatherly look on his face.

"Of course. Will they be coming alone, sir?"

"No. They have children. Their eldest girl is almost the age of my grandson. What a fortunate cosmic coincidence!"

Acknowledgements:

Special thanks to Simon, Marcia and Chisei.

FAIRIES

LITUO HUANG

Sept. 1993

Nelson's first memory began during his eighth birthday party. His classmates from third grade were playing on the lawn, their shrieks carrying through the kitchen window. He sat on a yellow chair, his legs dangling beneath yellow shorts. There was something wrong with him. A thin, salty crust had dried in the ditch between his nose and upper lip. When he wiped, the crust flaked onto his hand. He felt bad, very bad. Even his best friend, Cameron, who was two years older and as strong and good as Nelson was puny and bad, had given up consoling him. Cameron had finally told him to quit being a sissy before running back outside to play with the others.

Nelson slipped off the chair and paced the kitchen. The bad feeling grew into a big black mouth that swallowed him from the inside. He opened the refrigerator and saw the cake box his parents had hidden behind the leftovers. He opened it. A plastic Superman figurine stood with its hands on its hips, its cape blown sideways, on a field of white frosting. Nelson made a hole with his finger in the stiff, cold frosting and put the finger in his mouth. It was good, very good.

Half an hour later, Ken yelled at him. Maureen hugged him and put on the face she had when she was trying not to cry. The other children gave free vent to their grief. Even Cameron looked put out at the fact that there was no cake left.

"Why'd you eat that whole thing?" yelled Ken. "What is wrong with you?"

Nelson smiled. He had forgotten why.

Oct. 2015

In an illegally built cabin in the Mount Baker-Snoqualmie National Forest, a man sat on a foldaway cot next to a pile of discount-store picture frames. He was looking through a photo album. He turned over the cardboard pages with care and caressed the crinkly plastic protectors laid over the photos on each page. When he arrived at a chosen photo, he slipped it out of the plastic cover and laid it on the cot. Once he had compiled a small stack of photos, he began prying the backs from the frames. Outside, dew dripped off the needles of the Douglas firs.

Apr. 2016

Nelson was ravenous. His big breakfast had dissolved, leaving his stomach hollow. He could not concentrate on his too-bright computer screen. Closing his eyes, he repeated to himself: *What do I need right now?* This was his new girlfriend's pet mantra. He breathed in. *What do I need right now?* Breathed out. *What do I need right now?* He rolled his closed eyes. It wasn't working. This noise in his head wasn't susceptible to Zen. The only way to get away was to run.

Running had worked well for Nelson. The whole food thing was still a problem, but at least he'd finally lost the weight. He had always been the fat kid and he wasn't even funny. He had been irredeemably fat—but he'd shed that kid now. He laced on his sneakers and hit the trail heading east from North Bend.

At mile two, the trail turned into the forest. Nelson stepped onto a path littered with what looked like dead pine needles. The needles were slippery with fresh rain. He ran until his chest burned and his ears hurt from the cool air rushing past them. He could feel the blood pulsing in his head. He thought his heart might explode, that he might die if he kept exerting himself, and he liked the feeling.

Nelson lost track of the miles. He stopped. The forest surrounded him. Rain slipped off the fir needles and pattered onto the forest floor. He emptied his water bottle into his mouth. The water spilled over his lips and down the sides of his upturned chin, wetting his neck. He would be thirsty again later.

He jogged in a wide, slow circle, trying to find the trail. "Damn," he said, scuffing the wet needles with his toe.

He sat down and put his hands over his face. All the adrenaline had taken away his appetite, but he would crash soon. He was stupid for not having brought anything to eat. He walked over to a dense clump of trees, relieved himself, and prepared for a fresh attempt to find the trail. When he looked up, it was there, sitting in the crotch of a tree, eight feet off the ground.

It was a small cabin that looked like a gingerbread house. Even from the ground Nelson could see the big, overlapping shingles on the steeply pitched roof. The whole cabin was painted a dark brown the same color as the fir trunks. Branches, heavy with rain-soaked moss, arched over the roof. A wooden ladder reached from the ground to a landing that led into the small, dark doorway. There was no door. Nelson walked around the cabin. There were no windows.

Water dripped from the trees onto the ground, making a soft sound. He opened his mouth and a few drops fell onto his tongue. He tasted earth. He looked up at the toy-like cabin hidden in the trees. Leaving his empty water bottle at the bottom of the ladder, he began to climb.

Aug. 1993

A man walked through the door of Golden Page Comics, carrying with him a blast of hot air and a parcel wrapped in paper under his arm. He wore an apple-green jacket despite the heat. The cashier's nose was stuck in a comic and his head bobbed to the music coming out of his headphones. The man walked to the back of the store where two boys were hunched over the newest Batman release. He bumped the boys. His parcel fell to the ground and broke apart, spilling hundreds of cards. The taller boy jumped back. The short boy, whose skinny legs jutted out of his yellow shorts, bent down to help the man pick up his cards.

"Do you collect cards?" the boy asked.

The man looked at him. He looked at the boy's legs and dirty shirt.

"All kinds," he said. "Baseball cards, football cards, movie cards, art cards." He held up a handful. "Want to see?"

The short boy took one. On it was a drawing of a woman with green hair and butterfly wings. He held it up to his face. The woman was naked except for a sheet draped over her thighs.

"That's the green fairy," said the man. "By Mucha. He was a great artist." He scrutinized the short boy. "Do you like it?"

The tall boy looked up from his comic. "Art's for sissies."

"You're wrong," the man said, standing up and seeming taller than before. "Appreciation of art evidences a virile intellect."

The tall boy hesitated, frowning. Then he puffed air out of his nose and said, "I'm outta here." He punched the short boy, who still stared at the card, in the arm. "I said see ya."

"Okay, Cam. See you."

The man watched the tall boy leave. Then he stepped closer to the other.

"Do you like that picture?"

"I think so."

"Do you like art?"

"I like comics," said the boy.

"I do too," said the man with a rush. "But do you know what my favorite kind of art is?"

The boy shook his head.

"Photos."

"Photos are art?"

"They can be," said the man.

Apr. 2016

When Nelson had hoisted himself onto the landing, he nearly tripped over a rusty portable grill. He looked through the cabin's door-less doorway. It was dark inside. He stepped in.

A small plastic table, scattered with empty water bottles, and a military-type cot took up most of the cabin. Nelson tried not to bump anything as he moved around the interior. He had to stoop to keep from hitting his head on the ceiling. It was smaller inside than it had appeared from the outside. The air smelled like sawdust. Nelson got on his hands and knees to look underneath the table for water or food and felt a sharp pain in his left knee. His knee had landed on a screw that lay sideways on the gritty floor. He hopped up and was struck with dizziness. Bright shapes swam in his eyes and faded away. When his vision adjusted to the dark, he noticed the pictures on the walls.

There were seven pictures in all, five-by-seven photos in small frames. He picked his way around the tight interior of the cabin, peering in the low light. Each photo was of a young boy, bare-chested, looking up at the camera. Some of the boys were sitting, some were standing, one was kneeling, and one skinny, dark-haired boy was looking over his shoulder. The boys wore pairs of plastic costume butterfly wings over their bare backs.

Nelson's first instinct was to run. He felt the dark-haired boy looking at him through the frame with wide, expressionless eyes. Nelson felt nauseated. Some of the water he had swallowed earlier came back up his throat. It was sour. Thin, fresh saliva started to fill his mouth. A cold wind blew through the doorway. He backed against the wall and swallowed over and over.

As he was swallowing the last of his spit, he heard the ladder creak under a weight. On the landing, something metallic was knocked over.

"Someone in here?" The top of a bald head entered through the doorway.

Nelson stood up. His nausea vanished.

"This your water bottle?" A hand entered with a bottle.

Nelson wiped his mouth, his mind suddenly clear. He was ready. His memory ferried him the non sequitur of a road trip he'd taken as a teenager, of looking into a gem-colored lake and seeing through to the bottom. He walked through the doorway and onto the landing.

An old gentleman stood next to the toppled grill, wearing a faded green jacket. He looked at Nelson with a half-smile, half-frown that creased his short white whiskers. He held out the water bottle. Nelson reached for it.

"Didn't mean to disturb you," said the man.

"You didn't," said Nelson.

Nelson felt like he was facing a strange dog—not knowing whether the dog would wag its tail or lunge. He stood up a little taller. Green Jacket continued to smile curiously. They regarded each other for a few moments. The landing was small, and Nelson felt too close.

"This your place?" Green Jacket asked.

A long time passed before Nelson answered. "Yes," he said, with something like defiance. This answer seemed to relax the other, who looked down and smiled wider.

"Real sorry I knocked over your grill," Green Jacket said, stooping to right it. "This a nice place you got here. Pick-choor-esk." The way he said the word sounded like a piece of hard candy clicking against teeth.

Nelson felt Green Jacket toying with him. He was annoyed. He would not be toyed with. He would be master. "Come in," he said.

Green Jacket laughed through his nose. They went in. Nelson sat on the cot while the other man walked around the cabin, glancing at the photos.

"Quite the connoisseur, aren't you?"

Green Jacket stopped at the picture of the dark-haired boy and tapped his fingernail against the glass. Meanwhile, the drizzle outside had turned into a soft shower. He took something from his pocket. Nelson jumped up. Green Jacket started digging at the frame. There was a grinding, and a few seconds later, the tinkle of a screw hitting the floor.

"In fact," Green Jacket said, pushing the picture in its frame at Nelson, "why don't you take this?"

Nelson stumbled onto the landing. Green Jacket walked toward him, pushing him backward. The rain was cold. It soaked Nelson's hair and burned his eyes. He thrust the picture into his sweatshirt and scrambled down the ladder.

Sept. 2016

Nelson hadn't forgotten about the picture—he just wasn't thinking about it. Not thinking about it took more energy than he would have guessed. He didn't have any energy left over for work or to leave the house. He had stopped answering his girlfriend's increasingly annoyed calls. He spent his days walking between the fridge, the couch, and the bed. His sneakers were covered in fluffy dust. Maybe his pants didn't fit anymore—he wasn't sure, he hadn't tried.

It was on the evening news on a weekday. Some other hiker had found the cabin and they had arrested the owner. They didn't show his picture, but they reported that the man had been living in Mill Creek for forty years, in one rented apartment after another. His current landlady stated that he had been a model tenant.

Nelson turned off the television. He walked to the hall closet. He had spent so much time not thinking about what was in there, still balled up in the sweatshirt that was probably moldy, that it felt like opening the closet door in somebody else's home. He took out the crumpled sweatshirt. He felt inside for the frame, pulled it out, and laid it, photo side down, on the floor. The sweatshirt, disturbed, gave off a musty smell. He removed the photo from its frame. There was faded handwriting on the back:

Aug. 1993 – N.

Nelson pinched the photo between his fingers, walked to the kitchen, and burned it over the gas stove. Then he looked in the fridge.

NEST

ROSALEEN BERTOLINO

Iggy himself had high hopes that morning as he drifted out of the shelter and floated unsteadily through downtown. One hand clutched a paper cup of coffee, the other the frayed strap of his backpack. The shelter, rank with snores, bad dreams, and BO, was his least favorite place to spend the night. He preferred to sleep alone, behind the shrubs outside the post office at Third and D. But there'd been a rainstorm yesterday, the drops icy needles. The cardboard had melted. He was too old to be wet all night.

The storm over, Iggy squinted against the sun rising from behind the bank, the red glare of which felt like the throbbing inside his head, and studied the virtuous scurrying of people on their way to work. Today he would make himself a nest, he thought, not sure where yet, only that it would be cozy, safe, and just for him.

"Fuck you, Iggy," a voice called out from across the street. Iggy didn't need to turn his head to know who it was and he walked a little faster. His stomach was growling but no point now in getting in the breakfast line outside St. Vincent's. There'd been a misunderstanding over a pocketknife last night, sitting neglected on a bench, fair game. Everyone knew that anything so small and valuable needed to be kept on your person at all times. Iggy had only just slid it into his pocket before Guy had wrestled him to the floor. Fortunately, Guy was slow mornings and when Iggy glanced back there was no one behind him.

He was tired, not having slept well due to the snoring and the stink and Guy's clip to his jaw, still sore. He approached a quiet block of old mansions converted to insurance agencies and chiropractic clinics. The real estate office had an inviting portico, sheltered, with a thick welcome mat. He read the sign that the office didn't open until ten, tried the door in case someone had come in to work early. Locked.

He curled up, glad to be off his feet, leaning against his lumpy backpack. By his left foot was one of those prickly balls that fall off trees by the thousands in late autumn. By now it was winter, late December, almost Christmas, and the prickly balls were black and spongy. On the seedpod or whatever it was rested a tiny white spider. He'd seen a sci-fi movie once about spiders, giant ones, and another about a man who shrank to the size of an ant and was almost eaten by a sparrow. What if this seedpod was in fact a planet populated by intelligent beings that had landed here from outer space, and Iggy was the only one who could save them, only no one would believe him? That would make a good movie, he thought. He toed the seedpod and then squashed it with his foot.

Being inside the portico was like being in a movie theater, watching the movie of this particular day. An old lady, withered and bent, hobbled past with a pug on a leash, its back legs hitched to wheels, a kind of doggy wheelchair, so that the dog looked like a pull-toy. In his past life, Iggy had had dogs, all fine companions, great really, but he was wary of them now, even small ones like this could nip, and he didn't meet the dog's bulge-eyed gaze.

Now came two teenage boys walking side by side, not talking, their eyes intent on their phones, shutting out everything else, even each other, probably they were aliens and the phones portals to another world, their true home. Iggy was pretty certain that he, too, was an alien. He'd always been different, even as a child, confused by things that seemed obvious to his brothers, such as why you have to go to school when it makes your life miserable. He'd never been a good student. Perhaps it would've been different if instead of blackboards and letters they'd let him build a flying saucer. He felt the reassuring lump of his backpack, felt his eyes grow heavy.

Dreams—of winding tunnels, of chattering teeth, of large feet and a big blond man jingling keys, except, sadly, blondie was real. The man loomed over him and said, "This is private property. You need to leave."

Iggy was always being told to leave. Get out of here. Bug off. Scram. Even as a kid—his older brothers and his mom. Even his wife, his ex-wife, that is.

He took his time getting up, adjusting his shoes, the zipper of his pack. Blondie retreated a few steps down the sidewalk, gripping his cell phone, ready to dial 911. Iggy liked it when people became a little afraid. Always flattering to be considered capable of harm. "Have a nice day," he said to the man, who gave him a stingy little nod.

He trudged on, gunslinger in a Western, passing through town.

Past the Walgreen's and the taco shop and the Vietnamese nail salon, his knees beginning to ache, past the glossy auto palaces to the dingier, grayer part of town where auto body shops and mysterious warehouses clustered, past the vast littered parking lot of the bowling alley where he sometimes sneaked in to use the men's room. Once he'd found three full cans of Bud Light outside the back entrance. He scouted this area now, saw only fast-food wrappers and broken glass in the dirt, until he opened a tall metal dumpster and discovered an entire supermarket carrot cake, still in its clear plastic bubble. The bowling alley was popular for children's birthday parties but usually what was left were half-eaten slices of pizza and wadded paper tablecloths soggy with spilled soft drinks. He'd never had a whole cake to himself before; back in the life when he could have, it never would have occurred to him. He conducted an experimental lick of the cream cheese frosting, which was melty, sweet, and not a bit spoiled, then dove in, face first, the cake moist and crumbly, studded with morsels of walnut, pineapple, and carrot. He ate and ate, ate until he stopped tasting the cake altogether, until his belly hurt and his eyes watered. He needed to lie down.

Inside the dumpsters in this alley Iggy had at one time or another discovered large quantities of extra-thick cardboard, excellent for shelter, ham sandwiches still in their plastic wrap, a new pair of sneakers only slightly too large, and a black leather wallet (empty) that he'd traded for half a pint of Everclear.

Today, two of the dumpsters held only splintered crates and reeking bags of trash. When he lifted the third dumpster's heavy metal lid, however, he spied a jumble of beige carpet padding, soft and spongy, a ready-made bed.

Iggy propped the lid open with a discarded mop handle, tossed his backpack inside, hoisted himself up and over. Then, like a turtle in a shell, he clanged the lid shut. A thin seam of light leaked in along one side but when Iggy turned the other way, it was dark and perfect, and he curled into a ball. It was stuffy, but in a healthy way, like a sauna. He closed his eyes. The air grew warmer and he sucked it in in little sips. If he lived here, he'd drill a few air holes along the side facing the alley.

Suddenly the dumpster shook like an earthquake, and he was stabbed by sunlight and a scream. He didn't move, didn't open his eyes.

A woman called out, "Oh my God! A body! In the dumpster!" The lid clanged shut, a hideous, deafening sound, then flew open again.

"Looks like it's breathing to me," a man said.

Iggy didn't move a muscle; all he wanted was to be left alone. The two voices retreated, but the harsh white sunlight stayed. He heard snickering. "God, what if the garbage truck had come?" the woman said. "Then he really would be dead."

Iggy hadn't thought of that and his breath quickened a little. But he remembered that garbage trucks came only in darkness and not the broad light of day, and only when the dumpsters were wheeled out to the street. These people didn't know what they were talking about! He allowed himself to doze, a turtle on his back, safest just to play dead.

The whoop-whoop of a squad car. Cop voices. "A body, you say?"

"No, he's breathing. A vagrant." Iggy prickled all over; he hated that word. Something hard prodded his belly.

"Out! You're trespassing. This is private property."

Trash had a right to be in here but not Iggy. He wasn't even good enough to be garbage. Delicately, he wormed his way deeper into the bin, trying to sandwich himself between the golden layers. His eyes closed, he prayed. And felt himself ascend. It was the cops grabbing his skinny arms. They hoisted him out, tossed his backpack at his feet. "Get going," one cop said.

Iggy stood, weaving, on the sidewalk. He knew better than to disobey a police officer (having experienced the unpleasant consequences on numerous occasions) but his pride forced him to say, "I'm going to report you for abuse." Guy had taught this phrase to Iggy a few years ago and he'd found it useful ever since: it confused people, got them irate and tangled up.

The bowling alley employees, by now a crowd of four or five, muttered their disapproval. "Give me a break," one of them said. The two cops folded their arms tightly.

"You'll see," said Iggy as he began backing away.

He found himself on the frontage road, on the other side of the cyclone fences, the freeway traffic blasting past at a zillion miles an hour. He was alone, the afternoon spreading out before him like wide water, bright, relentless, and no shore anywhere, not that he could see. He might as well step in front of a truck.

Just as he was about to give up, he came upon a row of shabby pink Oleanders and in among them a quiet group of strange men. They were drinking from a bottle of vodka, passing it one to another in silence. Iggie was well-acquainted with those who made the local streets their home and he didn't recognize a single man.

"Greetings!" he said cautiously, and one of them beckoned him in under the shrubs and passed him the bottle. Iggy took a chug and passed it on. "Quite a storm last night," he said. Their strange eyes glittered but they said nothing. "Greetings from planet Earth," said Iggy. "Welcome." One of them, a burly guy, cuffed him hard on the shoulder. They stood all at once, handed him the bottle, and were gone. He took a few more invigorating chugs and stuffed the bottle in his pack.

By now it was late in the afternoon and, if he hurried, he could make it back to St. Vincent's in time for dinner. This was always a temptation, the food was good, but Guy might be there, still angry, and at this point Iggy was more sleepy than hungry, his midday nap having been rudely interrupted. He recalled the pleasant cushioning and warmth of the bowling alley dumpster. Businesses along the frontage road were beginning to close, their lights dimming, doors and gates locking. The people inside hurrying home. Iggy had done these things once. No more. He was retired now. Retired from everything. He enjoyed a little more vodka, and just like that, the sky was dark.

Iggy began thinking about a place to spend the night and while he thought, he walked. He remembered the intention he'd set that morning, of making a nest. Eventually he reached an elementary school. Usually he avoided these, so full of pitfalls—protective parents, earnest staff arriving early and working late, the night janitors—but this week everything was dark, it was the winter holidays.

He passed classroom windows to which paper stars and construction-paper snowflakes were taped. He washed up in an unlocked bathroom. The water was cold and the soap gritty; this filled him with a sweet nostalgia. He'd hated school but had loved being a child.

The dumpsters were behind the gymnasium. And what lovely dumpsters they were, locked up tight as a bank, all except one, into which Iggy carefully put his nose to check for rotten food, and then a hand, feeling for sharp objects. He touched paper, plastic; smelled paste, pencil shavings, and stale cookies. Nice nest, lovely nest. He climbed inside and lowered the lid slowly to avoid a clang.

He snuggled into bags of shredded paper, scrapped art projects. Shifting, he heard something that sounded like sifting peppercorns and that felt flat and scratchy. Glitter! Even in the dark, he could see the winking. He unscrewed the vodka, gave a toast to the glitter, and another, and another—to safety, good luck, good health, Merry Christmas and revenge on all mankind. He finished the bottle. Using his knapsack for a pillow, he slept. It became noisy and silent, noisy and silent. He slept through it all.

When Iggy finally woke, he was thoroughly rested and stiffer than he'd ever been in his life. He felt like he'd been flattened by a truck. He climbed slowly and painfully out of the dumpster. Peed a long, fragrant stream against the wall, the pee just coming and coming, puddling around his shoes. Belly grumbling, mouth cottony, beard long and grizzled, he walked toward town.

The sun barely up, the sky pearly gray, and the silence, which was like nothing he'd ever heard. No ocean roar of traffic. Not a single car, not even a bicycle. Judging from the height of the sun, the first seating at St. Vincent's was about to start and if he hurried he might make the second. But as he walked it became clear that the town was deserted. Not a single light in a house or store. Not a person on the street or behind a window. He saw a bobcat trotting confidently up Main Street. Shop after shop shuttered. A flock of crows flapped overhead. In front of the courthouse, where Iggy liked to nap on a clear, dry day such as this, a group of deer nosed the grass. Not normal. His heart thudded with excitement.

In the parking lot of the Smart 'N' Save, Iggy found a brick in the weeds and threw it through the tall window, which shattered musically, a cascade of safety glass. He waited for the alarm to sound. When it didn't, he stepped inside. Someone was already there, a woman he didn't recognize, with green hair and Army boots, clutching a bottle in each hand, baring her sharp teeth.

"More of that anywhere?" asked Iggy.

"Might be," she said. "These are mine."

"Sure are," said Iggy. He had no desire to argue. Her boots looked steel-toed. "Hey, what happened?"

She shrugged and left via the broken window.

The alcohol was in the back of the store. Iggy began filling a shopping cart, bourbon, gin, tequila, a bottle of triple sec (why not?), wine, wine, and wine, as he sipped from a warm can of hard cider. How good it felt sliding down his dry throat. The freezers were warm, the ice cream not just melted but moldy. In the Snacks and Household Goods aisle, Iggy snatched a couple of vinyl tablecloths to conceal his booty, which he intended to secret away somewhere, like a large squirrel. He crammed packets of peanuts and crackers into his pockets, tore the plastic off a sausage stick and put it in his mouth like a cigar. He touched a cash register just because he could, fiddled with the buttons, but nothing happened. Cake pans, whisks, cheap steak knives (he took a set), dish towels, can openers, microwave popcorn, granola bars, pillowy bags of marshmallows, fruit leather, yogurt raisins. All his for the taking if he wanted, and he did.

Of course, this upsidedown-ness meant that things in the wider world had gone terribly wrong. Maybe the electrical grid was down. Perhaps there'd been a mass evacuation. Perhaps the air was toxic. Maybe aliens had landed. Possibly himself and a few others were the only ones left on what might be a tiny ball to somebody or something in the universe. A thrill coursed through him, the chance to start his life over, by God, it was like a sexy girl all made of cake. "Baby, I love you," Iggy said, steering the overladen shopping cart out the back door.

Birds were singing. Deer were still nosing the grass. The best day of my life, Iggy said to himself, ready for whatever was about to come. He headed to the park for a lunch of marshmallows and gin.

So Amazingly Happy

Ellen Ricks

"Great, fantastic, I'm so amazingly happy!"

"Great, fantastic, I'm so amazingly happy!"

"Great, fantastic, I'm so amazingly happy!"

By the third try, Liza could almost believe that the words passing through her deep red painted lips actually had meaning.

"Just smile a tiny bit more and you're all set," she told the image in her bathroom mirror. She'd been at this for the better part of two hours. Spending time on her hair and makeup and taking meticulous care to radiate with pure joy. A psychic at a county fair had told her years ago that in a past life Liza had been an actress. In a way, Liza felt like she was an actress in her current one.

"Great, fantastic, I'm so amazingly happy!"

It wasn't a long walk from her apartment to her agent's penthouse. Not really, anyway. But

Howard, her fiancé, had insisted on picking her up.

"It's such a nice night. It almost feels like spring," she told him over the phone, a few hours prior. She had just gotten out of the shower, a black towel wrapped protectively around her.

"Honey, it will be late when the party winds down," Howard persisted. "You don't want to wander around the city on your own late at night. You don't want things to end up like they did the last time."

the last time.

the last time.

Liza gave an inaudible shutter. "I guess not."

"Good. I'll pick you up around seven. Love you."

"I love you too."

He was late of course, he was always late.

"Didn't keep you waiting long did I?" Howard asked as she slid into the passenger seat, careful to not have her black cocktail dress wrinkled in the process.

"Only a couple minutes." Liza smiled with practice ease. He had actually been twenty minutes and forty-five seconds late. But who's counting? Certainly not Liza.

"Sorry, I couldn't figure out which tie to wear. I never know what to wear to these things." He leaned to kiss her cheek, knowing full well not to ruin her lipstick.

She smiled. "Thank you darling."

"You must be so excited! I mean, this is it! It's your very own book on the *New York Times* Best Seller list! I'm so proud of you. How do you feel?"

"Great, fantastic, I'm so amazingly happy."

Howard gave her a large grin as he reached out to her, taking extreme care not to touch, or even go near, the long scars on her wrist. Instead he took her small, delicate hand, the one with the large opal engagement ring on it, and gave it a squeeze. "That's my girl."

He started the car, she stared out the window. Looking at nothing.

"Liza, beautiful! I've said it before and I'll say it again—you are a genius," Darrin Casey, head agent at the Mckenzie and Clark Literary Agency, greeted her the moment his dark eyes found her. Balding, clad in a cheap navy blue suit, a gin drink in his hand, Liza's agent held out his arms to embrace his latest sensation. "Bring it in here gorgeous."

Liza's eyes instinctively darted to the shiny hardwood floor. A blush crept across her cheekbones as she left Howard's hands and drifted into Darrin's arms. "You're too kind to me Darrin."

The agent gave a bark-laugh as he released her. "Too kind? That's the first time I've been accused of that!" Another laugh, drawing the attention of other party guests. A crowd started to form. "I'm telling ya, this kid right here is a genius. Brilliant, and I'm the schmuck that discovered her." There was a glint of pride in his tone, like he had discovered a country and declared himself king of it all.

"A lotta agents, lotta male agents, wouldn't understand this narrative. This point of view. But you don't need to have tits to know what the hell talent is. And talent is Liza Reed."

There were hums and nods of agreement from the onlookers.

Liza smiled. "Thank you Darrin."

He took a swallow from his glass. "Thank yourself darling. How does it feel to be a *New York Times* best-selling author?"

"Great, fantastic, I'm so amazingly happy."

Liza and Howard made their rounds together throughout the large penthouse. Liza smiled and made small talk but Howard did most of the talking, trying to do his own networking among the literary high and mighty as well as the up-and-comers. Liza wondered which category she fit into now, or if it mattered.

"Ugh, I can't believe this is their centerpiece," Liza scoffed when she saw it in the center of the buffet: the large sheet cake that looked exactly like the cover of her book. The black icing, in perfect cursive, spelled out *Girl in the Leopard Print*, along with the girl-in-leopard-print boots from the cover of the real-life book. Liza wondered just how many calories were in the frosting of the cake. How do you calculate the dietary makeup of a magnum opus?

"Wow, that looks beautiful, they must have gotten it from one of those fancy cake shops in the East Side or something," Howard remarked, hazel eyes wide with amazement.

"Do you think it's in good taste though?" Liza questioned.

"I'm sure it tastes great."

"No, I mean making it into a cake. It's a book about an eating disorder, who thought this was a good idea?" A bit of bile started to coat the inside of Liza's throat as anger, a small tinge of anxiety, started to build up in her chest. She swallowed them both down. "I just think it's kinda odd, you know?"

"I mean, it's the thought that counts."

Liza shrugged. Then, the poster caught her eye. "Oh God," she groaned, covering her mouth as she and Howard walked toward the monstrosity. A large easel in front of the buffet table held an almost life-size photograph of herself. Liza's book jacket photo that had been picked without her approval, without the many touch-ups she had wanted to add, that she needed to add. Now her dark eyes and her untidy dark hair were staring at her, judging her.

"That's a lovely picture of you honey," Howard cooed, kissing the actual Liza's cheek. But she could not be deterred from the sight.

"Ugh, it's all wrong! My face looks bloated and saggy. I'm twenty-six, how can my face get this saggy? And they didn't take the dark circles out from under my eyes, and, ugh, what the hell is up with my neck?" Liza continued to pinpoint and analyze every perceived flaw as Howard watched.

As she made her list, Howard's face slowly began to change. First love, then concern, followed by worry, a flash of fear, until it reached a cool anger.

"Don't." His voice came out firm, he was giving her a hard look.

Liza stopped mid-sentence and turned to her fiancé, flinching back at the intensity of his gaze. "Don't what?"

"You know what. Don't. Not tonight."

Liza flashed him a smile that showed teeth, an attempt to deflect. "I don't know what you're talking about darling."

"Look," he told her, placing his large, beefy hands on her narrow shoulders, forcing her to look into his pleading face. "You've been doing much better in the last few months and I'm so proud of you for that. But, you can't drop your basket right now. Not in front of all these people. Okay? You got to hold yourself together. Okay?" His words tumbled out of him like a wave, each syllable more desperate than the last. To Liza, it all felt like a knife wound.

It's his night, not yours. A voice echoed from the depths of her subconscious, trying to claw its way up to the surface. Liza had the good sense to push it back down.

"God, I thought you would be happy." It was the disappointment that brought her back to reality.

Liza brought her small hand up to his cheek and caressed it. "I am happy," she whispered, but the words felt hollow. She leaned over and kissed him, hoping to calm his nerves. To stop him from reliving her episodes.

He was smiling when they pulled away.

Like most of these parties for the YA flavor of the month, it was expected that the guest of

honor make the rounds and greet all the mov-
ers and shakers. For the first half of this tedi-
ous lap, Liza had Howard to lean on, but when
Howard got caught up pitching his chapbook to
an agent, she had to make the rest of the trek
alone. It all started to blur together:

"That must have been terrible. You must
have had a lot of willpower to stop eating."

"Why didn't you just eat a hamburger or
something?"

"Do you still see Edna?"

"Edna was such a fascinating character!"

"I know this is kinda wrong to say, but
Edna's my favorite character."

"You must be all right now."

Must I?

Liza could feel the temperature rising with
each question. Suddenly the walls were coming
too close together. She needed a drink.

The only mercy that befell Liza that night was
that the bar was open and there was plenty to
go around. Like a pirate finding treasure at last,
Liza stared in wonder of all the multicolored
bottles and shapes in front of her, unsure of
where to start first. Cautiously, she looked behind her to make sure that Howard was fully
occupied before she began; it had been five
months since her last drink.

After several minutes of fierce debating she went with a gin and tonic; nice and simple.

"Are you enjoying yourself Ms. Reed?" a calm, cool voice came from behind her.

Liza turned around to see the one and only Jeannie Brock, senior editor at Peacock Publishing. Her silvery hair, pulled into an elegantly simple bun, her teal boatneck dress was stylish and expensive. Ms. Brock was almost looking down at her through her large, tortoiseshell glasses with her sky-high heels.

Liza almost dropped her gin. Standing before her was the woman she both idolized and envied. Who, through the early years of her writing career, Liza had wanted to become, to impress. Now, she was gracing Liza with her presence. "Um, yes . . . . Ms. Brock, this is so great, fantastic, I'm so amazingly happy! And call me Liza!"

Jeannie Brock gave the younger woman a small smile, a knowing smile. "How nice. I'll be honest, I don't read a lot of the books that come out of Peacock. If I did, it would be a twenty-five-hour job. But, I read yours."

Liza's lips parted in a gasp. "Really?" she squeaked out.

"I mean, sure, I was going to put it in our YA mental health pile. But, it was different, the ending was different. So . . . vague."

"Yes, these illnesses aren't always so cut-and-dried and they don't just heal miraculously. It's a lifelong battle," she repeated her typical script, memorized from heart.

"I understand *Girl in the Leopard Print* was based on your life."

Liza could feel the beads of sweat on her forehead as her stomach started to knot. "Yes."

"Have you thought about what you're going to do next, after all of this is over?" she asked suddenly.

Liza swallowed hard. "I'm sorry?"

"Well the book is published, the tour almost over. It's all a success, but what next? I know Darrin is trying to sell you a sequel, but what more can you do with Edna? I mean, you wrote the book, you're about to be married. What's next for you?"

"I—" Liza had prepared a whole speech solely for this question, she had told it to many people at this party already. But confronted with this woman's cold green eyes, and her knowing smile, all of her prep work was lost. Liza took a long sip of her gin. "I don't know."

Jeannie nodded slowly. "I see."

"I'm sorry, I really must go. My fiancé is waiting for me. Thank you so much for everything." Liza turned to leave.

"Liza," Jeannie called after her. "Are you all right now?"

Liza stopped and turned to the woman she had admired since the start of her career, and felt her mask slip off. She threw her hands up. "I don't know Ms. Brock. But . . . I don't think it matters." She walked straight to the bar.

Liza finished her first drink and promptly got two more from Darrin, who conveniently forgot that he was not allowed to do that anymore. The words from Ms. Brock kept chiming like bells. *What's next for you? Are you all right now? Are you all right now?*

How did she know?

Heart racing, she looked to make sure that Howard wasn't around to see her and grabbed a bottle of gin from the bar and snuck into the bathroom. Click.

The bathroom spun before Liza's eyes, bringing up dry heaves in its wake. She could sense her control slipping with each contorted breath. Get it together, you have to get it together.

Are you all right now?

She stumbled over to the sink, gripping at the sides with both hands. Eyes darted up to the mirror overhead trying to find something, anything, in the image above that she could recognize as herself, but every time she blinked the figure in the mirror would change. Ugly, bloated bodies, saggy faces, tear-stained skin, every limb highlighted and distorted—until there was nothing but her in the mirror. Long dark hair, bright red mouth, there stood Edna, a skeleton draped in skin and black satin. "Hey baby."

Liza gave a long, defeated sigh. "Hello Edna."

"Missed me?" Her voice was soft, so syrupy sweet that it made Liza instantly nauseated.

"Not particularly," Liza mumbled, not making eye contact, to look at her would be a dangerous game to play.

"Well tough tits." She walked over to Liza, cold skeletal hand touching her cheek. "Mmmmm baby."

A chill shot through Liza's spine, she wanted to push the hand away. She wanted to march out of the bathroom and go home. Instead she leaned into the hand as Edna gently petted her. You shouldn't be here," she mumbled. "This is my night."

Edna laughed. "Oh right, I forgot. You're a celebrated writer. Authoress! Toast of the city! Tell me darling, what's it like at the top?"

"Oh it's great, fantastic, sooooo," her word drowned by the gin she swallowed. She tried to pull away but tripped over her sparkly heels, landing ass-backward on the marble tiles.

"Hey that's the spirit," Edna cackled, peering over Liza as she sat cross-legged on the counter top. "I would ask you to pour me a glass but we both know it's too many calories."

"I don't care about calories," Liza said defensively.

"Yes, and it shows."

Liza gritted her teeth. "Why the hell are you here."

"It's my party too, isn't it? Don't I deserve to bask in my glory?" She smirked.

"This isn't your party, it's mine," Liza told her firmly.

Edna laughed. "Of course it's my party. There would be no book without me. I'm the one who created all of this. All of you." Edna spread her arms out.

"Oh that's a pretty ring," Edna remarked, leaving her perch on the counter. She crawled over to Liza and into her lap. Liza could only watch in frozen horror as Edna took her hand to examine the engagement ring. "Who's the lucky guy? It's not Howard is it?" She laughed. "Please tell me it isn't Howard."

"So what if it is?" Liza whispered, her eyes trained on the floor as Edna caressed her around her torso; for a moment, she thought she was going to undress her.

"Look at you baby," Edna cooed, giving her a hard squeeze. "I'll fix that. It will be fine."

"You're not staying. You can't stay. I'm better. I'm trying to be better."

Edna laughed. "Oh come now Liza, don't be ridiculous! You can't not have me in your life. That's like cutting off your arm or your ear, or some dramatic shit. You need me." She caressed Liza's hair, gently tucking a strand behind her ear, leaning in to whisper, "You're mine."

"I don't need you," Liza growled, trying to push her off, rising to her own unsteady feet.

Edna's eyes flashed red. "Oh really? Look at you! Crying at your own party, no idea what to do for your future. Jeannie's right to ask you what are you going to do next because you got nothing else going on without me, without this. What? Did you think I would just go away as soon as you hit the best-seller list?"

Are you all right now?

"Let go of me!" Liza shouted. "I got rid of you once, I can do it again."

Edna raised an eyebrow. "Pffftt is that what you think? Is that why you haven't eaten in three days? Is that why you have a secret calorie app? Because you're the picture of well-ness?"

Liza opened her mouth, trying to think. Had it been three days? It couldn't be? She tried to remember but everything was fading in and out. How much did she have to drink?

Edna gently took Liza's chin so she had no choice but to look at her. "You have everything you ever wanted at your fingertips and you still cling to me. Because you love me."

Liza, heart pounding, picked up the bottle of gin, smashed it across Edna's face. She looked at Edna, waiting for her to feel any sign of pain when a lightning bolt of pain shot through her own arm, doubling over. She looked down finding blood, dark red, mixing in with the gin on the marble tile.

Are you all right now?

Edna whispered in Liza's ear: "Let me make myself perfectly clear: you are never going to get better."

***

"Jesus Christ," Howard cursed the second walked into the bathroom. With what little sense she had, Liza had managed to text Howard. "Goddamit, Liza."

"Hi," Liza called out from the floor, voice small and singsong like a child.

Howard's eyes went wide as soon as he saw her. "Not again."

"I'm sorry, I'm so so sorry." Liza's apologies poured out of her. "I don't know what happened."

"Hey Howie," Edna beamed, greeting him with a small wave.

"Dammit Liza. Why did you have to pick tonight to do this shit?" He stopped, sniffing the air. "Fuck, were you drinking gin?"

"I don't know. I'm sorry," Liza whispered, her uninjured hand clutching her temple, trying to make sense of what was going on.

"Geez, what an asshole," Edna commented, watching as Howard pulled Liza up by the shoulders and shook her enough to get her to look at him.

"Do you understand how painful it is to watch this?"

"Hey you can't touch her!" Edna shouted, pulling Liza out of Howard's grip and getting up in his face. "You have a lot of fucking nerve."

Liza watched the scene unfold from the sidelines, Howard and Edna going at it, angrily, violently. She could hear the high octaves of their shouting match but couldn't make out what they were saying, both of them sounding like Charlie Brown's teacher. She watched, feeling herself fade into the background, looking at her bleeding wrist. A slow alert bell began to ring in her head.

This is bad. This is bad.

"I need help," Liza whispered out. As soon as the words left her mouth, she was in front of Howard again, his face the image of disgust.

"You're goddamn right you do," he huffed, running a hand through his hair. "I thought you'd be happy. You said you were happy!"

"I tried."

"Did you?"

He slammed the door on the way out.

"What an asshole," Edna commented.

"He used to be nice," Liza mumbled. "Before I got ahold of him."

"If a guy talks about how nice he is, he's not all that nice," Edna told her, looking around the bathroom. "Honestly, he should have known what he's getting by now." Her eyes turned back to Liza, noticing for the first time that she was crying. She pulled a tissue out and handed it to Liza. "He secretly loves it, well . . . loved it. Especially the attention that the book got. I mean, that's why everyone's here, they all secretly love all this dark, mental illness shit."

"What?"

Edna smiled her cruel smile. "Baby, don't you understand? It's not you that they're here for. It's not you they love and adore and are holding a party for. Deep down, they all fall in love with me."

Liza looked at her, stunned. They all asked about Edna.

Using this pause as an opportunity, Edna grabbed Liza's hand and pulled her toward the door. "Come on baby, let's go greet our public!"

The door swung open and out stumbled Liza, disheveled, her eyes unfocused. She held her arms outside for her audience. "So you came here to see the mess? Well, look no further!" She let out a long cackle and tore through the party, knocking down tables, chairs, the awful life-size portrait of herself, leaving a trail of blood in her wake.

"Liza!" She vaguely heard Howard yell out to her along with Darrin's bark-laugh. But all of those sounds meant nothing to her as she got to the cake cover of her book and smashed it to bits, throwing pieces and chunks of it at the party guests.

"Look at her go!"

"Dear God! She's bleeding!"

"Is this what you want? Is this what you came here to see?" she screamed. As Edna smashed the poster, Liza's eyes spied the open window. I could end this.

On sparkly pink heels, Liza ran toward the window, opened her bloody arms and leaped.

"I'm so happppppyyyyyyyyy"

***

"Okay, so I'll admit, at first what happened at the party wasn't great. I mean, thank God for garbage day. But once the story got out, your book tripled in sales. There's even talks of a Netflix miniseries. I know how you feel about the movies. And I got some papers to sign for a sequel. I'm telling you, this place has got to be great material for your next book," Darrin told Liza across the plastic hospital table. "But we can talk more about that once you get out of here honey. Telling ya kid, your talent is unbeatable."

Liza said nothing, merely rubbing the bare skin of her fingers where a ring used to be.

"I mean. We're making the best of a bad situation. I talked to the doctors and they said you'll need to stay a few months, but I'll talk them down to a week or so. Then I'll get you all set up. You ever been to Palm Springs? Fresh air, the beach. Fix ya right up. You don't have to worry about a thing, okay?"

Liza nodded.

Darrin dropped the smile and looked at his client carefully. "How are you feeling kid? Like, really feeling? Are you all right now?"

It was Liza's turn to smile.

"Great, fantastic, I'm so amazingly happy!"
"Great, fantastic, I'm so amazingly happy!"
"Great, fantastic, I'm so amazingly happy!"

ABOUT THE AUTHORS

SARAH EVANS has had many short stories published in anthologies, magazines and online. Prizes have been awarded by, amongst others: Words and Women, Winston Fletcher Prize, Stratford Literary Festival, Glass Woman and the Bridport Prize. Other publishing outlets include: Unthank Books, MIR, Riptide, Best New Writing and Shooter. She has also had work performed in London, Hong Kong, and New York.

YOUSEF ALLOUZI is an author and data analyst who grew up in Texarkana, AR, but currently lives in the Pacific Northwest. He holds a BS in Economics and Masters in Public Policy from Oregon State University. His work has appeared in Scintilla magazine and OpenDemocracy. You can follow him on Facebook and Twitter @j_allouzi where he talks policy, economics, literature, and sports.

KAREN THROWER was born and raised in Oklahoma. She lives in Tulsa with her husband and their rambunctious five-year old. She graduated from The University of Tulsa with a bachelor's degree in Deaf Education. She is also a member of Oklahoma Science Fiction Writers and serves as the President and Facebook "Wizard" which she suspects has something to do with her young age. Her story "The Lost Ones" appears in the bestselling *Secret Stairs: A Tribute to Urban Legend*. You can find the rest of her works on her Amazon Author page: amazon.com/author/karenthrower.

JENNIFER PORTER lives in a big old house by a railroad track in a small, rust belt town. She was the co-founding prose editor at *The Tishman Review* during its existence. Her writing has appeared in numerous journals and anthologies including *Aquifer: The Florida Review, Fifth Wednesday Journal, Old Northwest Review, The Dos Passos Review, Apeiron Review, The Ocotillo Review, Chagrin River Review,* and *Nightingale & Sparrow*. She is writing a novel and is a graduate of the Bennington Writing Seminars.

ANNA O'BRIEN is a writer and veterinarian living in central Maryland. She is a contributing editor for the magazine *Horse Illustrated* and managing blog editor for the speculative fiction journal *Luna Station Quarterly*. Her fiction has most recently appeared in *Cheap Pop, The*

Ginger Collect, and *Blue Fifth Review*. She is a 2017 Pushcart nominee. She loves bicycles and dogs and bicycling dogs.

Originally from the idyllic coast of Maine, SARAH YASIN presently lives inland where she studies world literature in translation using the public library. A facilitator of writing retreats, she is also a convenience store clerk. She has stories in various literary journals, and her debut novella, *Retreat House*, has just been released. Learn more about her work at www.sarahyasin.com

EMAD EL-DIN AYSHA was born in the United Kingdom (25/11/1974) to Arabic parents. He is bilingual and completed his university education in the UK, attaining a PhD in International Studies at the University of Sheffield in 2001, with a BA in Economics and Philosophy from the same institution. He is currently residing in Cairo, Egypt and works in academic research, freelance journalism and translation, in addition to story writing. He was an adjunct assistant professor at the American University in Cairo (AUC), British University in Egypt, and Heliopolis University for Sustainable Development, and has worked fulltime as a columnist and translator for such newspapers as *The*

Egyptian Gazette and *Egypt Oil & Gas*, free-lancing with *Daily News Egypt*, *Mada Masr* and *Cairo Scene*. In 2016 he switched to writing science fiction and literary translation in earnest and joined the Egyptian Society for Science Fiction (ESSF) the same year. He has numerous online short story publications and has published in two (English-language) anthologies, *The Worlds of Science Fiction, Fantasy and Horror Volume IV* (in Australia) and *Trump: Utopia or Dystopia* (in Canada), followed now by Malarkey Books with an essay in another soon to be published anthology. He has published in three Egyptian anthologies for the ESSF and won Arabic-language prizes for his short stories. He has an SF novel in the works as well as a number of small SF series (Arabic and English) and is involved in writing academic papers and conducting interviews on science fiction and modern Arabic literature, with articles in such acclaimed journals as *Science Fiction Research Association (SFRA) Review* and *Foundation: The International Review of Science Fiction*, with more pending. He also published a syllabus on SF ("Science, Literature and Development in the MENA Region") with MULOSIGE (School of Oriental and African Studies, London University) itself inspirited by SF-related topics he taught while at the AUC. Next to science fiction his great passions in life are cinema (he's a movie reviewer as well) and history.

LITUO HUANG (@LituoH) lives in Los Angeles. Her work has appeared or is forthcoming in *JMWW*, *Bosie Magazine*, and the *Bethlehem Writers Roundtable*.

ROSALEEN BERTOLINO's fiction has most recently appeared in *Blood & Bourbon*, *Storyscape*, *New England Review*, and the anthology *Mexico Hoy!* Born and raised in the Bay Area, she is currently living and writing in Mexico.

ELLEN RICKS is a writer, Hufflepuff, and bisexual cyborg currently haunting Upstate New York. She has a BFA in Creative Writing from SUNY Potsdam which has been surprisingly useful. Ellen has been published creatively in *Capulet Magazine*, *Tiny Flames Magazine*, *Argot Magazine*, *Gods and Radicals*, and *Beneath the Rainbow*. She was the 2nd place winner in the 2017 Poetry Matters Project Lit Prize in their adult category. When not writing, Ellen enjoys drinking pumpkin spice everything and making terrible puns. Follow her on twitter @WithLove_Ellen and on Instagram at @sarcasm_in_heels.

Other titles from Malarkey Books

Teacher Voice, an anthology of fiction, essays, and poetry written by teachers, edited by Alan Good and DeMisty B. Dellinger

Forest of Borders by Nicholas Grider

The Life of the Party Is Harder to Find by Adrian Sobol

Visitor by Craig Rodgers

King Ludd's Rag, a magazine of long-form fiction

There's always plenty to read on our website: malarkeybooks.com.

www.ingramcontent.com/pod-product-compliance
Lightning Source LLC
Chambersburg PA
CBHW070258120726
47910CB00007B/2299